W9-BDR-175

WHERE DREAMS COME TRUE

The Daily Cruise Letter/The Daily Cruise News

Captain Nick Pappas and the staff of *Alexandra's Dream* are here to make your cruise vacation the experience of a lifetime. Our ship is a floating palace, and we do our best to make you feel like royalty.

If you enjoyed your visit to the islands of Corfu and Malta, why not consider a trip to Capri and the enchanted blue grotto? The shore-excursion desk located on the Athena deck will arrange your trip by hydrofoil from Naples. You'll discover why Capri is called "the most beautiful island in the world."

Once you're back on board *Alexandra's Dream* the enchantment continues. Unwind with a deep soothing massage in our spa, and don't forget to check out the display of perfumes courtesy of the world's finest fragrance companies. Then dress for dinner and enjoy an epicurean delight in the Empire Room, before dancing the night away to big band tunes in the Poseidon Lounge.

Mediterranean Nights…
Life doesn't get any better.

JOANNE ROCK

Two-time RITA® Award nominee Joanne Rock has traveled far and wide for the sake of her books, setting stories all over Florida, the Jersey shore, the Caribbean, Louisville, Boston and the Adirondack mountains of her home state, New York. Her thirst for writing a wide range of stories has driven her to write contemporary books and medieval historicals alike. Her works have been reprinted in twenty-two countries and translated into sixteen languages. A former college teacher and public relations coordinator, she has a master's degree in English from the University of Louisville and started writing when she became a stay-at-home mom. Learn more about Joanne and her work by visiting her at www.joannerock.com.

Mediterranean NIGHTS™

Joanne Rock

SCENT OF A WOMAN

HARLEQUIN®

TORONTO • NEW YORK • LONDON
AMSTERDAM • PARIS • SYDNEY • HAMBURG
STOCKHOLM • ATHENS • TOKYO • MILAN • MADRID
PRAGUE • WARSAW • BUDAPEST • AUCKLAND

ISBN-13: 978-0-373-38961-2
ISBN-10:   0-373-38961-2

SCENT OF A WOMAN

Dear Reader,

I took great pleasure two years ago in researching my first story set on a cruise ship—*The Pleasure Trip*. Set in the Caribbean, the book seemed like a great opportunity to talk my husband into taking our first-ever Caribbean cruise. I loved every minute of it! So you can imagine the wheels began to turn when I started work on a story set on a Mediterranean cruise ship. What a perfect chance to extend our travel horizons! Alas, we couldn't work out the logistics this time to take another vacation, but I can tell you I had a wonderful time playing the armchair traveler and exploring the Mediterranean through books, Web sites and conversations with people fortunate enough to live in some of these gorgeous places. I hope you enjoy this vicarious journey with me. For me, this is one of the most amazing powers of story—the pages of a book can take you virtually anywhere.

Thank you for joining me in this second installment in the MEDITERRANEAN NIGHTS series, and I hope you'll check out next month's release, *The Tycoon's Son,* by Cindy Kirk. Until then, bon voyage!

Happy reading,

Joanne Rock

To my bookclub—Jennifer, Elizabeth, Karen and Cathy—for sharing your ideas, stories, laughs and many bottles of wine with me.
Thank you, my friends!

DON'T MISS THE STORIES OF

Mediterranean
NIGHTS™

FROM RUSSIA, WITH LOVE
Ingrid Weaver

SCENT OF A WOMAN
Joanne Rock

THE TYCOON'S SON
Cindy Kirk

BREAKING ALL THE RULES
Marisa Carroll

AN AFFAIR TO REMEMBER
Karen Kendall

BELOW DECK
Dorien Kelly

A PERFECT MARRIAGE?
Cindi Myers

FULL EXPOSURE
Diana Duncan

CABIN FEVER
Mary Leo

ISLAND HEAT
Sarah Mayberry

STARSTRUCK
Michelle Celmer

THE WAY HE MOVES
Marcia King-Gamble

CHAPTER ONE

"YOU'D HAVE TO CASTRATE me before I'd spend the week on board a snobby cruise ship with a bunch of prissy perfume lovers," Adam Burns barked into the cell phone he thought he'd turned off the night before.

Sun pierced the blinds of his luxury hotel room even though the hands on his old-fashioned alarm clock showed the time to be six-fifteen in the morning. Since moving their corporate headquarters to New York from Los Angeles two years ago, his family had rented half the penthouse floor of a midtown hotel for living quarters. His younger brother—Adam's co-vice president at Burns Inc.—had a suite three doors down. Despite their physical proximity, Joe had woken him with a phone call demanding Adam take his place on a cruise halfway around the world.

"Castration is going to be a real possibility if you don't haul your ass out of bed and get on that plane. I can't go and Prestige Scents damn well needs a representative on *Alexandra's Dream*." Joe, the smooth-talking one in the family, had been scheduled to fly to Athens this morning for a fragrance conference on board a luxury Mediterranean cruise liner. "I spent last night in the ER by myself nursing broken ribs after a Jet Ski accident. Neither you nor dad picked up your freaking phones."

Ah, Adam thought. Maybe his cell phone had been turned off last night. He must have switched it back on when he plugged it in to charge. Guilt pricked his conscience straight through his hangover as he pried his eyes the rest of the way open.

A half-eaten room-service tray lingered by the couch while a handful of coffee cups remained on the cocktail table around an overhead projector he'd brought in yesterday afternoon for an impromptu meeting. He had to quit this breakneck pace. He didn't mind the business, but his personal life was such a disaster he'd been ducking all his cell calls for the past month.

"How many ribs did you say were broken?" Head still swimming from a friend's bachelor party the night before, Adam regretted staying out so late. What right did he have to toast the guy's upcoming nuptials when he wasn't even sure he believed in marriage? Long-term romantic commitments were too fragile to withstand real life in his opinion, which was why he limited himself to women who were looking for the same no-strings relationships.

Or at least, that's what he used to do when he had time. Lately he'd been working fifteen hours a day

to keep his father's vast network of business interests afloat. On the rare chances he had for some R
and R, he pursued fun with as much ambition as he
pursued a fat bottom line.

He'd been in relative hiding for the past couple of
months to duck a persistent female, so he'd jumped
at the chance for the all-male company of the
bachelor party. Hell, he'd gone to school on a football
scholarship. Darts and pool were his idea of a good
time.

"Three ribs," Joe repeated for emphasis, clearly
annoyed at his brother's slow mental processing.
"But the busted leg and the painkillers are the more
pressing reasons why I'm not getting on that plane
today and you are. Your Jet Ski female admirer is a
maniac on the water, bro. I'm not standing in for you
with her ever again, no matter how important she is
to the company."

Adam didn't argue the point. He'd been trying to
duck the up-and-coming actress for months after
she'd gotten the wrong idea about their relationship,
but the situation was sticky, since she was the face
of Prestige's newest perfume.

"You still there, Adam? I'm faxing you over my
notes on our goals for this cruise. There's a major
Dubai-based retail account up for grabs that you
need to secure before Dad retires and sends all the
Burns Inc. companies into a tailspin."

It had been a running theme for the past six
months: get their businesses in order before their

father retired. Jack Burns might overcommit himself in every area of his life—sometimes to the detriment of the company—but he was a dynamic businessman with a charismatic personality, and people trusted him to get the job done. There was sure to be a lot of upheaval when he vacated the president's seat.

A position Adam wanted no part of.

"Can't we do the deal directly? I could fly to Dubai tomorrow instead of tying up a whole week on a—"

"Not everyone wants to conduct business like a competitive sport, bro." Joe had used the same analogy a hundred times since they were kids. "Leave the New York attitude at home and seal the deal, okay? You owe me for yesterday."

Adam couldn't argue.

Crap.

He let his head fall back onto the pillows with a groan, realizing he was screwed. There was no point asking their father to go. The old man would lose his mind on a cruise ship—he hated feeling hemmed in. That was one of the reasons Burns Inc. held such diverse business interests. And the strategy had paid off, allowing the company to weather down turns in certain sectors of the economy. Fortunately, all the Burns men were very dedicated to increasing their earnings since a portion of the firm's profits went directly to breast cancer research. The cause had been the deathbed dictate of Adam's mother, a mission all the Burns men worked their butts off to fulfill.

"Fine. But I'm not spending ten days in a tuxedo." His brother and the perfume industry could just deal with it. "I can't believe you're making me go to a fragrance conference."

Of all the b.s. events. Their ambitious dad had dragged the family all over the world on business, and Adam had had more than his share of faking a good time at schmoozefests by the age of twelve. After his mother died, Adam had agreed to go into the family business only with the understanding he would never have to navigate corporate intrigue, make small talk with people he didn't like or—most important—perform for audiences in a penguin suit. He had the feeling this cruise was going to bust that deal on every front.

"Hey, at least you'll be safe from being stalked by Jessica Winslow and her publicity machine." Some of Joe's good humor returned to his voice at the thought. "And don't forget Prestige is Burns Inc.'s top-grossing company." Joe filled Adam in with a few details of his strategy, then signed off with a hurried, "Bon voyage, bro."

Clicking off his phone, Adam closed his eyes. Joe was right about escaping Jessica Winslow. The young actress believed her endorsement deal with Prestige included using Adam as arm candy. How ironic that after making millions of dollars for his family's company over the years, he'd gotten the most press from squiring around a spoiled starlet.

Hauling his butt out of bed, he slogged through

last night's dirty clothes on the way to the shower. Maybe some time away from the soap-opera drama his life had become would serve him well. Ten days on the Mediterranean wouldn't kill him. He needed to check in with the family's pilot once he drummed some of the hangover out of his head with hot water.

And then, by God, he'd do his best to pretend to care about perfume, and not just the dollars the Dubai account would bring to Prestige Scents and the higher cause those funds would finance. He shook his head at the thought of sailing around Europe with a bunch of fragrance enthusiasts.

It was going to be a hell of a day.

DANIELLE CHEVALIER forced herself to read over the conference itinerary despite the allure of the dazzling Greek countryside drifting by her penthouse balcony.

She was here to work, not play. And with her brother's parting words still resounding in her head, she wasn't about to prove him right by spending the whole cruise "sightseeing and daydreaming." She loved Marcel, but the man did not have a creative bone in his body, let alone a fanciful brain cell floating inside that financial mind of his. He would never understand that she could not bring any artistic inspiration to their exclusive fragrance company, Les Rêves, if she didn't let the world—sights, scents, exotic places—inspire her in turn.

Then again, she did not want her selfish need for creative recharging to be the cause of Les Rêves's failure this week when she sought their biggest account ever with a Dubai-based retailer attending the fragrance conference as an industry guest. She and Marcel had grown up in the business started by their mother, Monique, and they had inherited the Paris-based company jointly ten years ago. Danielle had thought it quite a coup when she was able to open a second store in Nice, where she now lived. But Marcel continued to grouse about the expense, failing to see the benefits of the business contacts she had made through the shop frequented by cruise line guests.

Of course, Marcel rarely saw anything her way. Their mother had named the company Les Rêves, meaning dreams, because she had always chased her dreams. Danielle shared the same starry-eyed outlook on life, but Marcel did not place much stock in dreams. He had long ago written off Danielle's contributions to the business as frivolous, even though her frequent ventures into the social milieu of European jet-setters accounted for a huge portion of Les Rêves's customers. Personal selling was her forte and came easily to her. She believed in her products with the same passion that she drew on to create them. But since Marcel had not seen a full return on her newly opened satellite shop in Nice, he had threatened to close the storefront unless she made up for her shortcomings by securing the Dubai account. Nothing like a little pressure for her trip.

"*Au revoir*, Piraeus," she whispered as the ship

sailed slowly past bright white houses perched on cliffs overlooking the sparkling azure water. It was no wonder the Greek flag featured those two colors.

Sighing, she turned her gaze back to the welcome packet in her lap, her wide-brimmed sun hat providing a thin slice of shade on the conference paperwork. Music drifted down from a deck above her, the cruise ship's welcome party by the pool, perhaps. She could have attended the fete, but until she previewed her personal business itinerary and the fragrance conference's meeting agenda for the week, she was not budging from her wide teak lounger. Not even for the martinis she had heard were all the more wonderful when made with fresh Greek olives.

Forcing her finger to skim down the list of conference attendees when she'd rather be salivating over the most beautiful coastline in the world, Danielle paused at the representative's name for Prestige Scents.

Joseph Burns.

Marcel had asked her to seek out the Prestige rep this week in addition to pitching the Dubai account, since the larger U.S. company had expressed interest in buying Les Rêves in the past. Danielle didn't want to sell the company her mother had worked hard to build—and to which she herself had dedicated the last ten years of her life—but she understood that it made sense to ensure Les Rêves continued to have an attractive profile within the industry.

The American businessman would be high on her

list of proposed contacts. And didn't that count as enough paperwork?

Bolting out of her deck chair, Danielle hurried inside to the suite's bedroom to find something to wear to the poolside celebration. Her brother might think she was too fond of parties, but since drinking up life firsthand was Danielle's greatest joy next to Les Rêves, she could see no problem in that. Besides, men did not understand that women in the beauty business ended up being walking billboards for their products. That also accounted for her need to have a certain wardrobe and to book a suite instead of the far more affordable stateroom. So much of her business was about projecting an image. Striking up conversations at parties had led to seventy-five percent of Danielle's customers.

Still, her conscience niggled, so she decided immediately to seek out the representative from North America's acknowledged leader in perfumes. She'd heard he was a smooth-talking businessman, but the rumor among a few of the boutique-style fragrance companies was that Prestige Scents had turned into a bloodless organization that knew nothing of its product since the Burns family had taken the helm.

Slipping into an understated sundress with a single poppy printed up the side, Danielle hoped to discover the truth about her competitor, if only to take some solace in the fact that she ran a company full of commitment and passion instead of a corporate business that spewed financial rewards and possessed no heart.

While she didn't mind being sought after by such a company, Danielle would certainly never sell Les Rêves to that kind of slice-and-dice operation, even if she could retire with a sizable fortune.

Contrary to everything her brother believed about her, she wasn't in business to play.

As she climbed the stairs up to the Artemis deck, Danielle felt herself relax now that she had a logical goal that would benefit Les Rêves. Inhaling deeply, she experienced the wonderful miniature world that would be her home for ten days, savoring the ambiance of *Alexandra's Dream* the way her mother had once taught her to savor all of life.

Her heels clicked rhythmically up the final steps, her skirt swishing pleasantly against her legs as an electric door opened at the top of the landing and a fresh breeze filled the stairwell. A young couple clutched each other's arms as they shared a bright yellow drink served in a glass the size of a fishbowl. They wore flowers around their necks, their giddy pleasure infectious as they laughed their way past her. But the sight also brought her a brief moment of pain, reminding her of her own former love and the sharp betrayal that had followed.

More eager than ever to join the welcome reception, Danielle hastened her pace, unwilling to let memories of Gunther cloud her day. She breathed in the intoxicating scent of the Mediterranean as they glided farther from Piraeus, the fragrance of the sea water clean and natural, stimulating her senses.

A small band played traditional Greek songs near a bar perched beside the outdoor swimming pool. She'd noticed on the ship floor plan that it was called the Coral Cove. At some point, the large swimming pool wound under the wall of caves at one end to become an indoor pool on the other side. But from this angle, she only saw faux rock covered with real plant life and a continual stream of water coursing down the stone facade into a mini waterfall above the pool. Some guests were in the water already, but most of the passengers milled by the railing, enjoying the scenery along the coast.

The perfume conference delegates were obvious in their more businesslike attire. They congregated in groups around a display of six-foot-tall perfume bottles that had been set up as a focal point for the conference attendees. Each sculpture was sponsored by a perfumer in attendance and was decorated by that company's creative team.

"Can I get you a drink, miss?" A handsome young server in a white uniform held a notepad in his hand, his accent hinting at Russian descent.

"Sparkling water with a lemon, *s'il vous plaît*." She would put off that martini for a little while to focus on business.

The server nodded and hurried away, leaving her to make her way to an empty spot at the rail. A soft wind blew her hair away from her face as she soaked up the moment, using all five of her senses to appreciate the day on every level—the way her mother the painter had said life should be enjoyed. Many per-fumers took the same approach, a fact attested to by the wealth of workshops offered this week on the connection between fragrance and the senses.

"Monique?"

An older gentleman in a pin-striped seersucker suit paused beside her at the rail, forcing his friend—a younger man dressed more casually in khakis and a black polo shirt—to stop beside her, as well.

She recognized the older man as Jonathan Nordham, the retired owner of one of England's few top-notch fragrance companies.

"It is Danielle, Monsieur Nordham," she greeted him easily in English, knowing she looked a great deal like her late mother, "and it is wonderful to see you. Are you attending the conference with your daughter?"

"Forgive me for my mistake, Danielle. You look so much like your mother when I first met her." He rapped his forehead. "My daughter says I live in the past more often than the present."

"I consider it a compliment to be mistaken for my mother, *monsieur*. And how is your daughter?"

"She's at home taking care of my first grand-child—at long last." A wide smile broke over his weathered face as he retrieved a monogrammed hand-kerchief from his breast pocket. "I don't tell her how to run the company now that I'm out of the business, but I can still lay down a few laws as a father, and I insisted she enjoy her time home with young Jonathan whenever she can."

The old man beamed with pride as he mopped his forehead beneath a white straw hat.

"Congratulations." Danielle spoke the word in the same breath as Monsieur Nordham's younger friend.

His younger, extremely attractive friend, she noticed. The man was tall with wavy, dark hair and blue eyes that could have belonged to a European, yet Danielle would bet her new fragrance line that the man was an American. There was a restless tension about him even when he stood still, almost as if standing still was an occupation that was foreign or uncomfortable to him. Danielle had noticed the same restrained energy in many of her American friends and business associates.

Although none of them were quite as wickedly handsome as this man, even in clothing that was decidedly casual for the perfumers' set.

"Pardon me, where are my manners?" Nordham shoved his handkerchief aside and made room for the server bringing Danielle's water. "Danielle, may I introduce Adam Burns of Prestige Scents? Adam, this fetching young lady is Danielle Chevalier, and she runs one of the most innovative and exclusive French fragrance companies on the market today. Les Rêves has been making organic scents since long before the current trend toward natural ingredients."

Shifting her glass of sparkling water, Danielle extended her hand.

"Pleased to meet you, Mr. Burns."

"The pleasure is all mine," he returned, squeezing her hand in a grip that was slightly more forceful than that of most European men.

Curious about why his name hadn't been listed as a Prestige representative, she found herself holding his gaze along with his hand. He looked vaguely familiar, although she was certain she would have remembered if they'd met. A woman did not forget such a sharp physical reaction to a man, and Danielle could count on one hand the number of times she'd felt that in her life.

Of course, as Marcel would be quick to remind her, each of those meetings had only hurt her in the long run.

"You are not Joseph." She didn't realize she'd spoken out loud until a short bark of laughter escaped Adam's lips.

Monsieur Nordham backed up a step.

"Will you young folks excuse an old man while you get to know one another? The heat is a bit much for me and I have heard rumors that there is an English tearoom on board."

"Certainly," Danielle assured him, realizing belatedly she still held Adam Burns's hand. She eased her fingers out of his palm and cleared her throat. "I think the ship map said the tearoom is on deck six. Maybe I will join you tomorrow?"

"That would be lovely." The older man was off with a wave, leaving Danielle alone with the entirely too good-looking Prestige rep.

"Don't let him fool you," Adam said in a conspiratorial whisper. "He needs to get out of the heat because he wants to access the flask of vilely strong alcohol in his jacket pocket. It's been twenty minutes since he offered me a nip and my throat's still burning."

She liked sharing this small secret with him, their lowered voices creating the illusion of intimacy. And yet, that sense of being able to share confidences had once tricked her into revealing far too much. Straightening, she resisted the urge to lower her voice.

"He offered to share his brandy with you?" She wondered if Adam knew what a compliment that was. "Monsieur Nordham must have been impressed with you—he guards his stash like liquid gold, no?"

"Really?" Adam moved closer to the rail, out of the flow of servers and passengers congregating near the buffet line that was snaking its way through the pool area. "In that case, I wish I hadn't lapsed into a fit of hacking."

"If you take tea with him, you can pour your nip into your Earl Grey to take the edge off."

"Ah. It pays to be an insider, I see." He leaned on the rail, his tanned forearms drawing her eye even more strongly than the Greek coast. "But since I'm a stand-in for my brother on this cruise, I have to learn all the subtleties of the fragrance industry for myself."

"Your brother is Joseph?" she clarified, more curious than she should be. But then, she told herself, her brother's directive was to seek out the Prestige rep. It was hardly her fault that he just happened to have the smile of a Hollywood movie star and the physique of a World Cup player.

"Joseph is my brother," he confirmed, catching her staring at his hands. "He called me yesterday to beg off this trip because of a few broken ribs and a busted-up leg."

With a wink and a smile he turned his attention from her to the miles of blue water refracting sunlight off every ripple. She was grateful he didn't seem inclined to press her into flirtation even though she'd been staring at him.

Then again, did that mean he wasn't interested? The moment of mild indignation she felt told her she had better set boundaries with this man. Fast.

"Many people would be thrilled to sail the most romanticized stretch of water in the world." She spoke English to Adam as she had to Monsieur Nordham.

All around them, however, a mix of languages could be heard as conference attendees found ways to communicate. During the workshops, information would be translated into English, French, Spanish and German so that everyone could be easily understood.

"The itinerary sounds great," he admitted, "but I'll let you in on a secret."

She would not let herself lean any closer to the enticing Mr. Burns. Not with the fate of her store in Nice on the line this week.

"I am listening."

"I know far more about the marketing of our product line than the actual fragrance aspect."

Now that was interesting.

"How perfectly shocking. I would not repeat that to anyone else here." She glanced over the small group of perfume reps that lingered by the display.

"Not knowing much about perfume is going to get me in a lot of trouble?"

"No." She turned back to Adam and was startled to see him staring at her intently. A little thrill shot through her before she remembered this attraction was a very bad idea. Unsure of herself, she kept talking to cover the awkward moment. "Your marketing knowledge would certainly be envied by this crowd, when so many of the old fragrances houses are sliding into bankruptcy. But to admit you do not know the finer points of perfume making? Sacrilege. Perfumers love their scents the way a vintner does his grapes and all their subtleties."

"I see." He nodded thoughtfully. "Maybe if you had time this week, you could share a little knowledge with me, just to get me through the cruise."

Spend more time with an attractive man in the same industry? She'd been burned once by trusting that business could be kept separate from pleasure and had jeopardized her company in the process. But she needed to cultivate a professional relationship with Prestige Scents as a security measure for the future of Les Rêves.

Danielle would just have to make sure her relationship with Adam Burns maintained certain boundaries.

"Actually, I planned to seek out the rep from your company for a meeting this week. Do you have time tomorrow?"

She could have asked anyone else on board for an appointment without flushing, but not Adam.

"You want a meeting?" He sounded a little surprised.

"Yes."

"I was thinking more in terms of a date."

She froze.

"What?"

"A date. You know, one man and one woman. We talk about each other instead of business." He gestured back and forth between them to stress the personal nature of his proposal. "Have fun instead of scrambling to impress each other with how many accounts we're servicing."

He paused, looking at her for a reaction, but she didn't have the slightest idea what to say. She was tempted. Lord, she was tempted. His speech fed into every "live for the moment" fiber of her being.

But she was trying to change that part of her nature.

"So what do you say, Danielle?" he pressed, his powerful body shifting ever so slightly in her direction. "Why not take a chance?"

CHAPTER TWO

HE SHOULDN'T HAVE made his move so fast.

Adam could see that he'd jumped ahead of himself when she'd asked for a meeting to talk shop. But he'd taken one look at her and *bam*. Danielle Chevalier was just the woman he wanted to end his two-months-long dry spell. The perfect candidate for a shipboard fling. Why couldn't he have just let the attraction take its course? He knew he wasn't the only one who felt the sparks.

"Unfortunately, Monsieur Burns, I take chances too often for my own good." Her killer French accent would turn on any man with a pulse.

But her words forced him to stop and think. Did a wild woman lurk beneath Danielle's sophisticated exterior? She wore her sundress with serious attitude. No flip-flops or blue toenail polish for this woman. Her strappy heels showcased pale pink toes while her slim dress tied around her throat to show off trim shoulders and a willowy figure. Glossy dark hair spilled down her back, and her lips were outlined in a soft red Cupid's bow, the color designed to catch and hold a man's attention. Although Prestige Scents had a small beauty division, Adam acknowledged that the tidbit about red lipstick was the sum total of what he knew about the cosmetics market.

"So you're a wild woman most of the time, but not adventurous enough to spend an evening with a clueless American who doesn't know brandy from grain alcohol?" Okay, that part might stretch the truth since he knew Nordham's stashed brew had to be something high-brow even if it tasted godawful. "I hear the observation deck offers a hell of a view."

He didn't know why he couldn't back off even when his head told him not to pursue a woman who wasn't interested in romance. But the urge to compete for her attention was too damn elemental to ignore and he couldn't walk away from the challenge.

"Is that right?" Lowering her head to sip her water, she seemed to hide a smile. "Do you speak of a view of the ocean? The stars? Or are you suggesting I might view you more favorably under the influence of both?"

A hint of her scent rode the ocean breeze, enticing him to continue this quest he didn't understand but couldn't stop.

"I don't mean to suggest I'll look any better, that's for sure. I'm more of a wysiwyg—what you see is what you get—kind of guy." He meant to retreat into more mundane topics, afraid she might take off if he pushed her further, then he found himself asking something very personal. "So tell me, Danielle, what kind of scent does a fragrance guru choose for herself?"

Judging by her swiftly changing expression, he could tell the question intrigued her as much as it did him. He might know little about fragrances, but he had the suspicion that Danielle's answer would tell him a lot about the type of woman she was.

She arched one eyebrow high as he absently waved away a waiter wanting to offer them appetizers.

"You cannot tell the overriding notes of my scent, *monsieur?*"

"Call me Adam." He wanted to get on a first-name basis with her, but he had to admit hearing "*monsieur*" roll off her lips proved a sensual experience all its own.

"You are unfamiliar with the components of my fragrance, Adam?" Her accent made the name sound exotic, the stress falling on the latter half. *A-dam.*

"I know you smell great." That was an understatement. What her scent did to him was way beyond P.G.

"I see you need my help more than I first realized." She turned away from the rail and their illusion of privacy. The captain's welcome reception was starting to break up as people returned to their rooms to dress for dinner. "I do not think I can accept the invitation for a date, but I would not mind taking in the sights at the observation deck after dinner tonight."

He wanted to push her to join him for dinner. And, yeah, he realized that nothing spurred him forward more than someone telling him no. But something told him to hold back when it came to Danielle. Adam was a born persuader. Marketing was his forte, and he knew he could seal the deal with the Dubai retailer with his eyes closed. But Danielle Chevalier posed a far more unique opportunity for…what? A midnight kiss? A few dinners? Something more? He didn't know.

But he did know he wanted whatever she might offer. Even if it was just the chance to smell her perfume again.

"That would be great. Should we meet upstairs on the Helios deck at ten-thirty?"

Nodding, she backed up a step toward the electronic doors leading into the stairwell and elevator bank.

"Ten-thirty." She spun on her heel and walked away, her sleek stride that of a woman who knew how to carry herself.

Hot damn.

If Adam could market himself half as well as he could market the goods and services that had come under the Burns Inc. umbrella over the last decade, he'd be wooing Danielle into much more than a few conversations about perfume.

"So I GATHER I would be able to sniff out individual ingredients in a woman's fragrance if I was a real perfumer, right?"

Danielle watched Adam settle into a deck chair

beside her from their quiet corner on the observation deck that night. When she had arrived, he had already tugged the loungers into an isolated space and had a bottle of Riesling with two glasses ready on a small table between them. For her part, she was grateful to leave the perfume conference behind for the night.

As much as she loved what she did, she had been seated next to a glass manufacturer at dinner and he'd talked for two and a half hours straight about bottle making, pumps and atomizers. Danielle thought she knew enough now that she could set up her own factory if she was so inclined.

She took her first sip of the wine while she thought about Adam's question.

"Perfume is like music, with layers of notes the discerning artist can pick out immediately in an elaborate composition. Because Les Rêves is particularly noted for its organic fragrances, our scents tend to be more overt and less synthetically layered, making it all the easier for a perfumer to detect the notes." She did not add that she took great pride in the layer of complexity they had achieved at Les Rêves in spite of their commitment to organic products. Their palette might be less extensive, but their array of scents within that framework was impressive.

"So I need to learn the notes first." Adam tipped his head back against his teak lounger and seemed to search the sky. He had removed his dinner jacket and his stark white shirt almost glowed in the pale wash of moonlight that played over them.

"When my mother taught me about scents, she took me in her garden and had me smell everything—the leaves, the petals, the bark of all the trees." The memory washed over Danielle with gentle joy. Her summers with *Maman* at the vacation house in Nice had been filled with painting and playing. Too soon she had realized that not everyone approved of having fun as a worthwhile way to spend time. "Those were the notes for me. Learning to recognize the bouquet of nature."

She sipped her wine, holding a mouthful on her tongue to savor each flavor before simply enjoying the harmony of tastes.

"Danielle, would you excuse me for just a minute?" Adam sprang to his feet, setting his wineglass on the table beside hers. "Literally a minute. No more."

"I will not time you," she declared, amused at his desire for speed. "A French woman does not need a stopwatch to measure increments of life."

"Excuse me." He spun on his heel and stalked away to the stairs leading down to the main lounge.

Danielle tipped her head back to count the stars, dazzled by the night sky spread above her as if for her pleasure alone. She had barely gotten herself oriented to the constellations when Adam returned, a big bouquet of flowers in hand.

"Oh, no." Shaking her head, she smiled. "You did not swipe flowers for a private lesson, did you?"

"I rented them for an hour with twenty bucks and a promise to bring them back." He set the glass vase on the table between them, moving the wine bottle to the floor to make room.

"There is not much here aside from roses." Sitting up to explore the bouquet, she turned so that her feet rested on the floor. "You are familiar with the scent of roses, no?"

"Definitely." He nodded. "But let me take a smell to remind myself."

He leaned in close to the flower and breathed deeply. The vase was packed mostly with pink roses and pink tulips, but there were a few other flowers woven in with the greenery around the edges.

"The bell-shaped flowers are tulips," Danielle said. "Their fragrance is much more subtle, but we use them sometimes."

"And this?" He held up a sprig of white flowers with greenery.

"That is chamomile."

"Like the tea?"

"Exactly. Although the scent is different when the flowers are fresh."

She identified the remaining flowers and blooms for him and then took another sip of her wine while he sniffed away.

"All right." He closed his eyes. "Test me."

"You think you are ready for a quiz so soon?" She admired his commitment to learn something about the business he represented and wondered if he pursued everything in his life with such intensity.

Now, peering at him in the moonlight, she decided

there was something intriguing about a man with his eyes closed. Danielle toyed with the idea of waving her fingers in front of his face to make sure he was not peeking. Or maybe it would be more fun to lean near him, her lips close to his.

The thought sent a shiver down her spine. Plucking a bloom from the vase, she shook the stem gently to remove the excess water and then held it inches from his nose.

"You're being too easy on me," Adam scoffed. "That's the rose."

"An expert already then?" She pulled a fern out from underneath the layers of flowers and held it close to his face. She waved one hand behind the plant to generate a small breeze to carry the scent to him. "Then what do you smell now?"

"The fern." He didn't even hesitate.

"You are cheating," she accused, convinced a novice would not have been able to pick that one out.

He opened his eyes, no trace of guilt on his handsome face.

"I didn't cheat by looking." He took the fern from her and sniffed it again. "But I knew you would think the greenery was the toughest to gauge so I figured that's what you'd go for when you wanted to stump me."

"That was very clever of you, Adam, but it hardly improves your scent education." Danielle watched him turn the fern around and around between his fingers before he used it to fan her face.

"Yet it continues my education in marketing, which is all based on psychology and the consumer mind-set." He stopped fanning to look at her. *Really* look at her. "The more I understand how people think, the easier my job becomes."

His unadulterated stare was as intense as the rest of him, and Danielle felt something shift between them. The chemistry she had sensed from the moment they met now became much more evident. The social niceties they'd hidden behind earlier fell away to reveal an intense awareness of one another.

"So you believe you know how I think?" Danielle retreated behind her wineglass, needing to break the powerful connection. How could she let her guard down so easily with this man?

Adam Burns was her competitor in a business that guarded its secrets jealously. She would do well to remember that, especially when he seemed to be reading her mind already.

"No." He tucked the fern back into the vase, slightly off center from where it belonged. "I couldn't pretend to know how you think about most things, but from your tone of voice or your expression, I can sometimes make small predictions about how you'll act or what you'll say."

"Even having just met me? I think you are wrong, Adam Burns. Women are not so predictable. You cannot forecast their thoughts like the weather."

"I've offended you."

"Of course not," she denied automatically, wondering how someone who seemed so brash could be that intuitive. Because despite her denial, his words had touched a small nerve. She'd been well played by another man in the past. "It is just that no woman wants to think a man can anticipate her reactions. A woman wants to be darkness and mystery to a man's sunlight and heat. The sexes should be like yin and yang, no?"

"But if a man can't begin to understand a woman, how would he ever make her happy?" He appeared genuinely perplexed and she regretted that her past had insinuated itself into her thoughts.

But then, how could she separate herself from all her life experiences? She couldn't help that her past colored the lens through which she saw the world. No one could.

She sighed.

"I do not pretend to know the right answers," she admitted. "I only know the ones I do not like. I have precious little experience with what makes a man and a woman happy together."

"Then let's toast to something we share in common." He raised his glass and placed her in her hand. "Here's to mutual ignorance when it comes to romance."

Clinking her drink to his, she echoed his toast and drank deeply. He charmed her in spite of her best intentions not to be swayed by a man in the same business as hers.

"It occurs to me we might wish to draw some

boundaries around our business relationship before we continue lifting our glasses in a more personal sense." She wouldn't make the same mistakes twice. "Perhaps we should discuss just enough business tonight to be sure we will not be stepping on each other's toes this week."

"I'm game." Adam's gaze followed another couple who were leaving the Helios deck, arms wrapped around each other. "Did you want to stand by the rail for a better view?"

Nodding, she stretched to her feet and brought her glass over to the side of the deck. They were all alone in the observation area, at least for the moment.

"It is a beautiful ship." Danielle turned back to see the proud smokestack behind them bearing a circle of silver with gold stars.

The spa and fitness center were up here along with a driving range and tennis courts. The hot tubs at midship were a popular destination tonight, and she could see a couple kissing in the closest sunken tub. The sight made her wonder how long it had been since she'd been kissed that way. The memory was a bittersweet one since the man she would have shared her last kiss with had hurt her.

"I met the captain today after you left the welcome reception. Apparently *Alexandra's Dream* is newly refurbished."

She'd read that somewhere, along with the fact that the ship had been named after the owner's late wife. The tearoom was supposed to have a portrait of Alexandra Stamos and Danielle planned to see it tomorrow when she met Monsieur Nordham. Elias Stamos must have loved his wife to name this big, beautiful vessel after her a decade after her death. The thought touched Danielle, perhaps because she still missed her mother so much.

"We could not have asked for a more decadent setting for the fragrance conference." Her cocktail-style dress flapped against her calves in the breeze off the water, the silk teasing her skin. "May I ask what business you hope to accomplish while on board?"

She didn't know how the companies might help each other, but it was worth investigating since Prestige had made an offer on Les Rêves in the past.

"I'm here to secure a deal with the Dubai retailer," Adam said. "Joe thinks we need a greater presence in the United Arab Emirates and a contract there would bring in substantial new revenues."

Danielle's heart sank. They were no longer competitors in a general sense. With Adam's declaration, she realized they would be vying for the same piece of lucrative business this week.

"It seems we will be in direct competition then, because I am here for much the same reason." And although she was not afraid of the competition, she had to admit to a twinge of disappointment that Prestige wasn't looking at business possibilities with an elite French import like Les Rêves.

"You're pursuing the Dubai account, too?"

"*Oui.* And I guess that should come as no surprise to either of us since the promise of business there is profitable to say the least. No doubt many of the other fragrance houses aboard will make a similar pitch."

"So you're not upset that we'll be competing?" He turned toward her, his body blocking her from the breeze for a moment.

She caught a hint of his scent and was taken aback by the blend of hyssop and cedar and another note she couldn't quite define. The desire to lean closer and inhale was strong. But damn it, why did they have to be vying for the same account?

She needed to present a strong front.

"Why would I be upset?" Her thoughts about Adam were taking a much too personal turn. "Do you think you have the account all sewn up? I have to admit I think I have the advantage over you when it comes to perfume, even if you did correctly guess the fern."

"That's good news." He looked down at his leg and she realized the fabric of her dress had blown around the back of her legs and the purple silk now clung to his trousers.

She tugged the material away, flustered even though she had no real reason to be.

"Danielle." Adam touched her arm and she looked up from her wayward dress to his face.

The expression in his eyes didn't surprise her. She had sensed the attraction there earlier, yet she hadn't been prepared for the heat of it. Never had a woman's elbow felt like such an erogenous zone.

"This could be complicated." She didn't need him to spell out what he wanted because she saw it too clearly in his eyes.

"What if we keep business separate from pleasure? We don't talk about our work, we just—"

"My work is who I am. If I tried to talk to you without talking about my business, I would be giving you a woman who wasn't Danielle Chevalier. Don't you see?"

"I'll tell you what I see." He stepped closer, claiming a corner of her personal space as his own. "I see a ten-day cruise stretching out in front of me and the opportunity to enjoy it with a woman who's smart, entertaining and sexy. That's ten days, not a lifetime commitment. So I ask myself, why not make the most of that time until the real world calls again? Why does it have to be more complicated when we know it's going to end on the pier in Barcelona?"

She tried to form an objection but it was difficult now that he stood so close. His very presence had her swaying toward his point of view.

The spicy scent of him seduced her as surely as his strong, masculine build. Hadn't he charmed her with his bold-talking American ways? His willingness to admit he knew nothing about perfume had caught her off guard and made him different from other men, who, in her experience, liked to bluff their way through any situation.

Heaven help her, she couldn't say no.

"How could we possibly hurt each other in a mere ten days?" she said. The answer was they couldn't, right?

But Adam approached the question from a different direction.

"I think it might be more to the point to see how much pleasure we could bring to each other in ten days." He reached to capture a stray strand of hair blowing across her cheek. The warm strength of his hand along her face churned a tenderness deep inside her.

This was dangerous ground to tread with Adam. It was one thing to find shared pleasure. It was another to discover tenderness and mutual regard. Memories of Gunther assured her the latter was far more dangerous.

"Shall we toast to pleasure seeking?" she said finally, powerless to halt whatever magic lurked between her and this man. At least she could control her response to it.

"No." He shook his head, his hand cradling her cheek as he tipped her face to his. "I think this is the kind of agreement one seals with a kiss."

CHAPTER THREE

ADAM DIDN'T WANT to scare Danielle away by being too intense so he couldn't kiss her the way he wanted. He knew he'd never craved a woman this deeply before, and he sure as hell wouldn't lose the ground he'd gained with her by pinning her to the rail and kissing her senseless.

He tried to remember what she'd told him about perfume—that you had to appreciate the individual components to fully appreciate the harmony of the whole composition. With that in mind, he savored the silken feel of her cheek beneath his hand, the delicate throb of her pulse as he trailed his finger down her slender neck.

Surely he could slow himself down enough to enjoy those individual facets.

"Your intentions are noble, *monsieur*," she whispered through the darkness as she wrapped her hands around his neck. "But I think we should not waste time, lest I change my mind."

His heart slugged harder at her words as realization dawned. She didn't want to savor individual notes. She was ready to explore the whole range of sensations working together.

Arching up on her toes, she rose to meet his kiss. She kissed like an angel, light and graceful in his arms, making him want to squeeze her tighter so she didn't get away.

"Danielle." He spoke her name between kisses, breathing the word over her mouth like an invocation.

Everything about her seemed dark and exotic, from her violet eyes to the seductive French accent that he would hear in his sleep tonight. He hadn't planned on involving himself with another woman for a while after the debacle back in the States with the actress who had misconstrued his motives when he'd squired her around New York a few times. He'd tried to set her straight gently, but she'd threatened to withdraw her endorsement of Prestige's newest perfume. Although the company could find another "face," the publicity would be negative.

But his decision to back off dating for a while had been made before he met Danielle. She had the kind of allure that made it easy to break rules.

"I must say good-night." She pulled away, speaking softly. "Perhaps we can spend some time together tomorrow after you finish your meetings."

When she glanced behind him, he realized another couple had come up to the raised observation deck. Still, he couldn't make himself release her.

"Come ashore with me tomorrow." He would set up something with the Dubai retailer later in the week. Right now, his top priority was to make the most of this time with Danielle. "I've never been to Corfu."

Gently he combed her hair off her shoulders and felt it ripple down her back.

"You are not alone. I hear it is a gorgeous port."

"How about we meet at eight o'clock?" He thought the ship docked around 7:00 a.m.

"Unlike you, I have to work on this cruise in addition to play. How about we meet at noon instead? That will give me time to make my apologies to Monsieur Nordham since I won't be able to meet him for tea now. And I do have a meeting with the Dubai company rep tomorrow."

He realized the account must mean a great deal to her and he hoped she wouldn't be too disappointed when he firmed up an agreement for Prestige by the end of the cruise. He'd already set up an appointment with Ahmed for later in the week, and from his brief phone call to the rep, Adam felt confident he understood what the retailer wanted to see in a presentation. Besides, there was no way he'd let himself fail. Joe had charged him with only one business goal at a time when all of Burns Inc. was in an uproar over their father's inevitable retirement.

For years Joe and Adam had let their father take credit for getting business done that they'd accomplished for him. Neither of them looked forward to dismantling the myth of Jack Burns, and despite all the good they'd done for their family's foundation, neither son wanted the top spot that would soon be vacant or all the stress that came with it. Adam and Joe had already sacrificed too much to become embroiled in company politics and the inevitable infighting that would follow their father's departure. A behind-the-scenes role suited Adam just fine.

"Noon it is. I'll wait for you down by the disembarkation deck."

She backed out of his grip, taking her warmth and effervescent spirit with her.

"Very well." She plucked her wineglass off the floor as if to return it to the bar. "But I hear the temperatures can sizzle this time of year. I hope you can take the heat."

She winked at him before turning on her heel and walking away, leaving him staring at her swaying hips. As much as he admired the view, he hoped it wouldn't become a common one, since he much preferred the sight of her walking toward him.

He'd be ready for a hot day tomorrow. In fact, he was counting on it.

"HAVE YOU TOUCHED base with our contact at International Markets? Ahmed?"

Danielle rolled her eyes, knowing her brother Marcel could not see her on the other end of the phone as she lay on the bed in her suite.

"Marcel, how rude would I be to demand attention from a business associate who already agreed to meet with me tomorrow? I set this meeting a week ago and there's not a chance I'd break it or do anything to jeopardize the most important piece of business I'm here to conduct." She might be enticed by the chance to spend time with Adam, but she wouldn't botch this deal that Marcel insisted was crucial to their continued success.

Les Rêves meant everything to her, and she trusted her brother's instincts when it came to the company's finances.

"Right. Will you give me a call tomorrow to let me know how it goes?" There had been a tense edge in Marcel's voice for the last few months and it came across now despite the hundreds of miles between them.

"Actually…" she hedged, unsure how Marcel would feel about her having a personal life. Then again, why should she apologize when she hadn't dated for almost two years? "I'm going ashore at Corfu with a new friend tomorrow, so I won't be able to call until quite late."

She rolled to her back on the white coverlet, waiting for the worst of his lecture to subside. He trotted out stock phrases about her love of partying and her need to take life more seriously, then he moved to his central theme lately of needing to bring in more business. But what hurt the most was his closing statement.

"You'll need to provide the name of this new

'friend' so I can run a routine background check on the guy, Dani. I'm not going to have a repeat of your last boyfriend now that we've just started recovering from the damage he did to earnings."

Anger roared through her, hot and quick.

"How dare you?" Sitting up on the bed, she tossed aside the decorative pillow she'd been holding and paced the floor. "After all I've done to bring Les Rêves back in line—all of the accounts I have hand sold to make up for that loss—how can you have the nerve to suggest I would ever let someone like that into my life again?" Memories of Gunther's betrayal still stung even two years later, but not because he'd broken her heart. No, she'd gotten over that hurt long ago. But she hadn't been able to repair all the damage he'd done when he stole a valuable perfume recipe and marketed it more cheaply by using inferior ingredients.

"Just give me the guy's name, Dani." Marcel sounded beyond weary, but she was still so angry she could hardly speak.

"Because my judgment is tainted for the rest of my life now? I have lost all ability to form opinions about people because I was wrong once?"

"If you trust your judgment, why does it matter if I check him out? Are you afraid I'll find something we should be concerned about?"

Danielle sighed, not liking her brother very much at the moment. They'd always been very different people, but never more so than when it came to the future of Les Rêves.

"His name is Adam Burns. He is a VP with Prestige Scents and, yes, he is competing with us for the Dubai retail account."

"You realize you're not the only one with a livelihood at stake here, right?" Marcel had done the books for Les Rêves for as long as Danielle had been the company's public face. They'd always disagreed about where to take the business, but never as often as in the last few years.

"Yes, I realize. And you should know I would never do anything to jeopardize the future of our very loyal staff." She fumed for another moment before sliding into an armchair, exhausted at treading old ground. "It is not fair to beat someone up for the same mistake forever, you know."

"It hasn't been forever, Danielle. It's been two years, and even though you want to forget it, I promise you the accounting ledgers remember all too clearly. Have fun in Corfu, but if there is anything remotely suspect about Adam Burns, I'm going to ask you to make a decision in the best interest of Les Rêves."

The thought darkened her mood, which had been flying high after the kiss she'd shared with Adam earlier. Would Marcel find any reason she should stop seeing a man who intrigued her so completely?

"Fine." She had told Adam that she and Les Rêves were inseparable and she meant it. The company her mother had started with a dream and a few plants in the backyard was Danielle's first priority. "Good night, Marcel."

"So TELL ME what you know about the Burns family."
Danielle sipped her tea at a table with Monsieur
Nordham late the next morning after convincing him
that tea could be taken any time of day in the Rose
Petal, the ship's English-style tearoom.

Although a more formal high tea would be served
later in the day, the Rose Petal offered finger sand-
wiches and scones until the dining rooms opened in
the evening. Danielle settled into her chintz-covered
chair and sipped from the delicate floral teacup. The
ginger-peach tea was a far cry from Earl Grey, but
very soothing. Her nerves were still upset after last
night's phone call with Marcel, so she had decided to
do a little investigating of her own between workshops.

"First you must tell me if you are interested in the
business profile or what I know of the family personally." Nordham smiled as if he'd already guessed
the answer. His aristocratic aura lingered in everything from the silver ring he wore bearing an etching
of his family crest to the unassuming studs in his
French cuffs.

"Actually, I wonder what you might know of the
family personally." She saw no reason to hedge with
a man who'd always expressed open admiration for
her mother and her tendency to live life to the fullest.

"I know more about the younger brother, Joseph,
who is apparently the more polished of the pair.
When Prestige Scents debuted their new line in
London last year, Joseph made the rounds of high-

end retailers to ensure placement the same time I toured those shops myself."

"But this is the first you've met Adam?" She hoped the more she found out about Adam and his family, the more relaxed she would be when they spent time together today in Corfu.

Her last error in romantic judgment had resulted from ignoring warning signs that something was amiss. Fancying herself in love, she'd discounted any rumors she'd heard that suggested Gunther wasn't all he seemed.

"I struck up a conversation when I caught him trying to stack the hors d'oeuvre meats into a club sandwich," Nordham explained. "He claimed he was food deprived after a long flight, but I gathered later that he'd arrived by his family's private jet so I don't think the poor chap could have suffered too greatly, do you?" Nordham poured himself more tea from the individual pot. "He has a great fondness for brandy, I discovered. I had to replenish my stock after he joined me for a nip."

Danielle hid a smile.

"So the family must be very wealthy." She knew many people with money new and old, but private jets were a luxury that traditional wealth couldn't always afford.

"Burns Inc. has interests all over the world. Prestige Scents is a moderately sized piece in a vast global pie that makes Adam's father one of the most successful men in business today."

The news sat well with Danielle. Why would

Adam attempt some kind of corporate espionage to undermine Les Rêves when his own companies had met such a level of success?

"How do you think Adam's prospects are with International Markets? Any better than ours?" She knew Nordham would be pitching to the Dubai retailer, as well.

"Only six companies have been invited to give a presentation, you know." Nordham lifted his teacup to the genteel-looking older woman playing the harp who had just paused between songs. "I think contracts will be awarded to at least two of those, so the odds are decent for all of us. Prestige's advantage is that they bring a lot of star power to the table with all the Hollywood endorsements they seem to garner."

Danielle hadn't really considered that edge, but then she'd been so confident in her own secret weapon that she hadn't given much thought to scouting the competition. She'd spent weeks analyzing scents native to the region to infuse her fragrances with authentic touches, and her specialty line of Arabian Nights perfumes was going to dazzle the Dubai retailer.

"How did your meeting go this morning, by the way?" Nordham asked, clearly taken with the harpist. He couldn't seem to drag his eyes away from the elegant, silver-haired woman dressed in crisp white linen.

"It went well." Danielle was certain she'd impressed Ahmed with her ideas for the themed line of scents, which would be sold exclusively to International Markets. Even the packaging was a departure from Les Rêves's signature pink-and-gold boxes. The Arabian Nights fragrances were tentatively slated to sell in jewel-toned bottles with Moorish style boxes, the whole collection as colorful and varied as a walk through a Middle Eastern marketplace. The retailer had liked her concept but had asked her to go deeper and see if she could make the marketing more specific to the region. She'd agreed to meet with him once more before the cruise was finished. While she didn't usually invest so much time on an account without a contract, exceptions would be made for the Dubai account since it represented a potentially lucrative untapped market.

Danielle would go the extra mile to sketch some ideas for packaging and promotion.

"Ah, I sense a secret selling point or two in there," Nordham teased, finally turning his attention her way. "Well, I wish you luck, my dear. But for now I must hurry you on your way since it's already noon and I happen to know you have another date awaiting you."

She settled her teacup back in the saucer, all the more eager to see Adam now that some of Marcel's concerns had been settled to her satisfaction. Adam Burns didn't need to steal secrets from Les Rêves when he stood at the helm of one of the world's most successful fragrance companies. Her gut instincts about him had been accurate.

"You spoke to Adam this morning?" She gathered her purse and handed Nordham his cane.

Nordham refused the walking stick with a shake of his head.

"No offense, my dear, but I'm going to see if I can fill your seat with another beautiful woman as soon as that attractive musician is done with her set. And, yes, I saw your young man this morning. I discovered he likes his eggs over easy, but he's not much for brandy in his coffee. Have fun, Danielle."

She kissed his cheek before turning to leave. On her way out she hurried past the painting of Alexandra Rhys-Williams Stamos. The willowy blonde with delicate features looked perfectly at home in the tearoom, but Danielle's fanciful nature thought she spied a hint of steel in Alexandra's blue eyes.

She nodded in greeting to the painting, confident Alexandra's spirit must be happy to have had her dream fulfilled so lovingly in Argosy Cruises' refurbished ship. Danielle hoped she would be able to carry out her mother's dream as successfully. Les Rêves was the passion of Monique Chevalier's life, and Danielle refused to do anything to jeopardize its future.

But as long as Adam Burns proved to be the man she believed him to be, Les Rêves was not at risk.

Danielle continued to believe that right up until the moment she spied Adam.

She had expected him to be standing there waiting for her. She hadn't expected him to be wrapped in another woman's arms.

CHAPTER FOUR

"JESSICA?" Adam had to angle back to identify the woman who had practically tackled him on the gangway in Corfu, the woman whose arms were still glued around his midsection.

He'd only stepped through security in case Danielle had thought that's where he'd meant for them to meet—

Danielle.

With renewed determination fueling his efforts, he pried Jessica Winslow's arms off him and stalked toward the gangway where ship security checked passenger identifications going on and off *Alexandra's Dream*.

"Did you see a woman—" he began, but just then he spotted the back of Danielle's head on the other side of the check-in point.

"Danielle," he shouted, digging in his pocket for the ship ID he'd had a moment ago when he disembarked. "Wait."

She turned, hesitated. Behind him, Jessica tugged

on his hand while one of the ship's security officers asked them to move aside to allow passengers to exit.

"Aren't you surprised to see me, Adam?" The actress who had caused him so much trouble pulled him backward even as Danielle continued to walk away, deeper into the ship and then out of sight.

Adam was about to chase her down, but first he needed to clear something up with the Hollywood starlet who couldn't seem to understand no.

Damn it.

Jessica had gone too far this time. Hiding out from her clearly hadn't worked, and had resulted in his brother's broken ribs. If Jessica didn't want to work with Prestige Scents, so be it. But he was drawing some serious boundaries with her starting right now. Allowing himself to be led a few yards away from the ship, he spotted a stone bench near the dock and gestured toward it.

"I sure as hell am surprised. Can you sit for a minute?"

"I can't believe you sent poor Joseph in your place when we went on the Jet Skis the other day. Since you wouldn't come to me, I figured I'd come to you. I start shooting a movie in Italy later this week so I thought I would drop in on you—"

"In Corfu." He couldn't believe this woman—all of twenty-five years old—had chased him around the globe.

"Isn't it wild?" She blinked up at him with wide brown eyes, her gold necklace winking in the sun.

"I had my assistant dog your brother until he told us where you were hiding. I think his pain meds were kicking in when she finally got him to spill it."

She looked absurdly proud of harassing an injured man. And that's when Adam realized he couldn't afford to waste time with small talk. This woman might have ruined more than just his day ashore with Danielle. She might have jeopardized the whole cruise.

"Jess, I don't know where you got the idea that we were more than business associates, but I have a…girlfriend aboard this ship and I—"

She stood, oblivious to the hundreds of people filing off the ship into the ancient Greek city for a day of shopping and sightseeing.

"You have what?" Her voice dropped to an icy stage whisper and Adam congratulated himself on saying the right words to finally snag her attention.

Even if they weren't quite true.

"A woman I care about. A woman I don't want to mess things up with." That might be stretching it, but he was willing to push the truth to give Jessica a face-saving out—now.

From somewhere across the street a lightbulb flashed. Tourists taking pictures? Or had Jessica simply planned another publicity event? Damn it, he hadn't thought about that. She baited cameras wherever she went.

"And just what does that make *me*, Adam? The woman you dated to secure a celebrity endorsement?"

Oh, that was priceless. Apparently he was going to be treated to the full force of her acting abilities today.

Her raised voice reminded him how much she enjoyed an audience, and two guys he'd hoped were tourists now swarmed closer with their cameras. Great.

"Jessica, I took you out a few times to show you Manhattan because you asked me to." He fumed inside, knowing this woman had planned her trap with all the prowess of a lifelong hunter. "I'm almost fifteen years older than you and it would never have occurred to me that you wanted anything more than a chaperone. I've got to meet someone on board the ship now and I think you should know that I'm going to let Joseph handle your work with Prestige from now on so there's no more confusion between us."

Standing, he debated the wisdom of sprinting for *Alexandra's Dream*. But then, his desire to avoid her had landed him in this position in the first place.

"Who is she?" Jessica didn't move an inch, stiff and regal in her new role as the woman scorned.

Lord, she was going to make one hell of an actress.

"No one you know." And with that, he gave in to the urge to cut and run. The fact that he'd upset Danielle mattered to him more than he would have thought, and he felt the need to protect her.

"You realize I might withdraw my support from Reckless perfume?" she threatened from behind him.

Not damn likely.

Adam knew Jessica loved the money as well as the status she would derive from the multimillion-dollar ad campaign for the new fragrance. There wasn't a chance she'd turn her back on the deal.

"Just let Joseph know if you don't want to promote the brand anymore," he shouted back, showing his ID to ship security so he could board.

His brother was going to kill him.

But it wouldn't matter as long as he could convince Danielle he wasn't the two-faced jackass he appeared to be.

WHEN HE FINALLY FOUND Danielle, she was seated at the wine bar on deck six, her dark hair knotted into an elegant twist that showed off the delicate back of her neck. Relief flooded his veins after almost an hour and a half of searching the ship and ringing her room, dodging people from the fragrance conference who wanted an appointment with him.

The relief didn't last long, however, as he realized she was engaged in a conversation with a tall foreigner who bent his head to hers to catch every word she spoke.

He had no right to be jealous of the man in wire-rimmed glasses and charcoal suit that had to be custom-made. Yet there it was—a sharp pang of envy for the guy who stood close to Danielle.

"Excuse me?" He joined them at the bar before he'd fully thought out what he was going to say. He nodded to the other man before turning to Danielle. "I've been looking for you and—"

"Ahmed, have you met Adam Burns of Prestige Scents?" She cut Adam off with her sweetly spoken introduction, gesturing to the other man to include him in the conversation. "Adam, you know Ahmed Ramnathan of International Markets?"

Aw, crap. This was the UAE retailer he was supposed to be impressing this week and Adam had just interrupted the guy. He recognized the man's face from his business bio now.

"A pleasure to meet you, Ahmed." Adam shook his hand and reminded himself to thank Danielle profusely for saving his butt before he rattled on in front of the guy about standing her up. "I believe we have a meeting later in the week."

Only then did Adam notice the perfume bottles on the bar. Had the two of them been discussing Danielle's fragrances when he interrupted them? She'd hate him forever if he'd messed up her chances with a major account.

"Indeed we do," Ahmed confirmed in unaccented English. "I am glad to meet you in person ahead of time. Danielle and I were just sharing our thoughts about a few of the new brands being launched this year." He looked down at the bottles on the bar and tapped the top of a familiar magenta-colored stopper. "We are both impressed with your new Reckless brand."

"It's delightfully subtle and surprisingly fresh,"

Danielle added, her manner flawlessly professional despite the fact that she had to be annoyed with him for what she'd seen on the pier in Corfu. "I like the direction your brands have taken in the last five years."

They spoke easily for a few minutes about the new research director at Prestige's laboratory and Adam wondered how he could excuse himself from the conversation so he wouldn't take away from Danielle's time with an important contact.

But then the conversation turned abruptly as Ahmed picked up another bottle, this one labeled "Obsidian."

"And what of Zumer's newest scent, Adam? Did you find it pleasing?"

Damn. Adam smelled a trap with the question, though the other man's face gave nothing away. He had no idea what the perfume might smell like or what the industry consensus on the launch might be, but he did recall the Zumer brands were affordably priced and the company had posted growth in the last two years.

"I think they know their market." Adam glanced over at Danielle, who sat listening intently. "You can't argue with two years of growth."

"Unless you begin to rush your products to market." Danielle set down her wineglass and retrieved the perfume bottle, removing the stopper to sniff the blend. "I think there is a risk involved when you are held accountable by a board of directors to show unceasing profit. Occasionally the creative process requires more time to develop."

Danielle passed the bottle to Adam and he took the required sniff, wondering if he'd ever get her alone today to apologize. It was bad enough falling backward into a conversation with a contact he needed to impress, but Danielle's inevitable confusion and disillusionment pricked at his conscience.

"I can't speak to how women will like it," Adam said honestly, "but I can tell you this much—the name was poorly chosen."

Ahmed frowned as he adjusted his glasses and read the name on the bottle again.

"You do not like the name?"

"Not sexy enough or sweet enough. It should be one or the other, as long as it projects an appealing amount of femininity." As soon as the words left his mouth he experienced a moment of panic that the fragrance was a cologne for men and he'd just revealed the depth of his ignorance.

But neither Ahmed nor Danielle contradicted him. Instead, Ahmed nodded slowly.

"There is tremendous power in naming," he acknowledged, looking at Adam with new respect. "I will hope for Zumer's sake this is not their first misstep, but I will watch the fragrance's performance with interest in light of our discussion. For now, I must leave the two of you to attend a workshop on new trends in pheromones."

He gave a short bow and departed, leaving Adam

alone with Danielle at the bar. The afternoon crowd was thin, with most of the regular cruise ship passengers on shore in Corfu. Many of the attendees of the fragrance conference were still on board for a handful of afternoon workshops, which were starting shortly, so the bar was quiet except for a piano player in one corner of the room.

"Thank you." Adam knew he needed to apologize to Danielle for what had happened on the pier, but first, he would thank her for helping him out with Ahmed. "I'd never met Ramnathan in person and I was so focused on finding you, I didn't make the connection when I first saw him."

Danielle held up one of the perfume containers to the light. She seemed to inspect the golden liquid before replacing the tiny decanter on the bar.

"I believe it is best to play fair, even in business, although I know there are many who would not agree." She was wearing a simple strapless dress and shrugged her bare shoulders. "When I secure a contract from International Markets, my conscience will only let me enjoy it if I have not purposely hindered the competition."

He wondered if she meant that as a warning to him. Did she think he would cheat in this race to win Ahmed's business? No doubt what she'd seen earlier had swayed her opinion of him. A man who was dishonest in his personal life would have no qualms about slippery ethics in his professional life.

"I respect that and promise to abide by the same

principle." He stared into her violet eyes and hoped his gaze communicated his sincerity as much as his words. "Danielle, I need to explain to you about what happened out on the pier."

"So you're saying she flew all the way around the world to see you and she was so thrilled she suffocated you in an octopus hug, and yet the two of you have never dated?" Danielle didn't bother to conceal her skepticism.

After seeing Adam with the beautiful young woman, Danielle had ditched the disembarkation deck and headed for a lecture on classical antiquities in the library on the Bacchus deck at one o'clock. But she'd been restless and agitated despite the entertaining talk, remembering what she'd seen on the pier. Finding Ahmed at the bar nearby had been a stroke of good luck, giving her a chance to socialize with the rep for a few minutes before Adam arrived.

And while Danielle had been tempted to excuse herself from the bar at the same time as Ahmed, she wasn't a pouty child and knew she should give Adam a chance to explain.

Now, sipping her ouzo in deference to their Greek port, she waited for Adam to respond to her question.

"Haven't you ever met people who would do anything for a little extra publicity?" He shrugged and shook his head. "Maybe it's a cultural thing. In the States, everyone wants their fifteen minutes of fame, and some people will push it for as many minutes as they can grab."

Danielle felt a pang of recognition. She'd never sought the public spotlight, but she'd been born into a well-known, wealthy family and knew how easy it was to attract attention.

"My father has made a career of marrying high-profile women with money to spare." She turned at the sound of clapping outside the wine bar. The lecture must be finishing up. "I guess that's kind of similar. You must be quite the—how do you say?—quite the prize catch to elicit such attention."

"Far from it." He denied the charge so vigorously she wondered why it offended him. "I'm thirty-eight years old and all I do is work. As I walked onto the ship yesterday I realized this is the first time I've taken anything close to a vacation in a decade."

"But from this young woman's perspective, you are wealthy and successful. Combined with a face that is compelling enough, you make an enticing prospect."

"I told her my brother will have to handle her relationship with Prestige from now on. She threatened to pull her endorsement of our new scent."

Only then did Danielle remember seeing the actress's face in a racy ad for Reckless perfume in which she bared her midriff and covered her hips with the sheerest of scarves. The image had appeared in a two-page spread of a popular fashion magazine.

A moment of fresh jealousy seized her. She

hadn't realized her feelings for Adam had such a possessive bent.

Warning bells blared in her head.

"Adam, I believe you are sincere about not having a relationship with this woman. But I would rather not date a man who is being chased by females I would be tempted to beat off with a stick. That would not be good publicity for any of us."

His laughter was so warm—so genuine-sounding—she felt tempted to join in. What was there about laughter that could chase away bad feelings and leave such a marvelous warmth in one's heart?

"I think you'd be able to walk around without your stick. And we've only got nine days left now." He peered out the window at the town of Corfu on the island of the same name. "I really wanted to spend today with you."

And she really didn't want to get drawn in by a man in the same business, especially one involved with Hollywood starlets, no matter the circumstances.

"I would rather not risk a run-in on Corfu today," Danielle admitted, reluctant to risk getting caught up in Adam's personal life drama and lose sight of her professional goals.

If they were going to forge ahead with a week of fun together, she'd make sure she protected herself at the same time.

"We would probably avoid Jessica if we caught up with the tour sponsored by the fragrance conference," Adam suggested. "Or we could just stay on board." He nodded at an officer with four stripes on his crisp white uniform.

"Why don't we take a look at the antique replicas on display in the library? I heard part of the lecture about the pieces earlier and the speaker was very enthusiastic about his collection." That kind of date would involve less pressure than a full-blown day spent touring a romantic Greek port. Besides, she wasn't dressed for playing tourist any longer, her high heels an impediment to traipsing around town.

Adam peered toward the library, dubious.

"Okay. But I have to tell you I'm about as well-versed in antiquities as I am in perfume."

"Not to worry." Danielle finished her ouzo and signed the credit slip the waitress had brought. "I want to look strictly for inspiration. Viewing any kind of art makes me feel closer to my mother."

She walked out of the wine bar and Adam followed.

"Danielle, wait." He caught her elbow and turned her toward him before she reached the library.

The warmth his touch inspired surprised Danielle. Even though he had women chasing after him halfway around the world, she was still disarmingly attracted to Adam Burns.

"Yes?" She hoped her answer sounded cool and controlled, because even if she still wanted him, she would never make a show of it the way his starlet did.

At least, not until she was more sure of his trustworthiness.

"I'm really sorry if I made you uncomfortable earlier. That definitely wasn't the way I wanted to greet you on our first chance for a real date." His blue eyes were troubled. Intent.

"I do not offer trust easily, Adam, but I will trust you this once more since I have been the victim of bad timing before myself." Awkward moments could happen to anyone, right? Still, a sliver of unease slid up her spine.

"Thank you." He lifted her hand to his lips and planted a kiss on the back of her fingers. "I'm going to make it up to you."

She could not deny a thrill at the feel of his lips on her skin, but she forced herself to simply smile as they continued toward the library.

Two men played chess at a wooden game board just outside the library, while inside the warm-colored woods gleamed in the sunlight streaming through the windows.

Bookshelves lined the walls, and comfortable chairs invited reading. The scent of leather and paper relaxed Danielle as she entered, another testament to the power of smell. She had read all the studies that proved the scent recognition center for the human brain was situated near the one for memories. That proximity accounted for perfume's ability to evoke strong emotional reactions, since memories were tagged with scent associations.

"Welcome." A tall brunette with pretty blue eyes and a fashionable pair of reading glasses rose from her desk to greet them as they walked in. "The library closes at 4:00 p.m. this afternoon, but feel free to browse until then. I'm Ariana Bennett, your librarian. Just let me know if I can help you find anything."

"Thank you." Danielle returned the woman's smile, noticing a dictionary of ancient Greek on Ariana's desk. "We are just going to look at the reproductions from Father Connelly's talk."

"Of course."

Was it Danielle's imagination, or did the librarian's smile tighten just a bit? She had heard there was some tension between the original American crew members who had remained with the ship and the staff hired by Argosy Cruises, the new owner. But then, Danielle knew both Father Connelly and Ariana were Americans. Perhaps she'd imagined the librarian's reaction.

"There are cheat sheets," Adam called over to her in a stage whisper from the middle of the library. He was pointing to a glass display case filled with replicas. "Bingo."

Danielle passed a special section of science-fiction and fantasy "feature reads" to join him, her eye drawn to a half woman, half cat statue that she hadn't seen during Father Connelly's lecture. The animated priest from the Midwest had been affable and entertaining, but Danielle had found herself longing for a few more dates and details on the pieces. Maybe the cheat sheets would answer her questions.

"What about this one?" she asked softly, not wanting to disturb the two other library patrons who were reading in opposite corners of the room. Ariana Bennett was back at her desk, bent over her Greek dictionary and a notebook.

"Ah. Don't you recognize—" he looked down at the notes near the silver statue "—the famous Egyptian cat goddess, Bast?"

His imitation of a stuffy professor made her laugh despite her desire to stay quiet.

"No, I did not. I guess I will leave that up to the expert in the field. What kind of goddess is Bast? Fertility?" The statue had the body of a woman and a feline face.

"Apparently its significance is disputed, but it suggests here it was a protector goddess and had the face of a large, predatory cat before history corrupted later incarnations to take on domestic cat features."

Danielle could not deny a small sense of connection with the figure. "Life does tend to beat the fierceness out of us sometimes."

"I don't know about that. Maybe we just learn how to control our fierceness so we can channel it more effectively." Adam stood near her, close enough that she could sense the warmth of his body. Their proximity called up the physical attraction that seemed to lurk close to the surface whenever he was around.

"Have you learned to channel your passions?" As soon as she asked the question she realized that it sounded suggestive. "I mean, do you think you've managed to harness your ambition and dreams into smart goals for the real world?"

"My dreams have been on a short leash for so long I'm not sure what they are anymore. Yeah, I guess they're damn well harnessed." He reached to toy with a lock of her hair that had come loose from her chignon. "What about you?"

She couldn't feel his hand on her hair, but knowing he touched her had a powerful effect. Her breath caught in her throat.

"I find it a challenge to restrain myself sometimes." Putting her feelings on display had cost her dearly.

"I envy you." Releasing her hair, he turned back to the artifacts.

But Danielle was more interested in his words than the collection in the display case.

"It is not fun going through life with regrets for your mistakes." She took after her mother in so many ways, but she'd never inherited Monique's ability to shrug off her failures as easily as she rejoiced at her successes. After losing so much to Gunther's betrayal, Danielle could not afford to lose her store in Nice, as well. In fact, she'd started the shop in Nice specifically to escape Paris, where Gunther lived. Nice represented many things to her heart in mind. Her freedom. Her independence. Her determination to promote Les Rêves—her dreams.

"But at least you give yourself the freedom to make mistakes." His jaw hardened, a muscle flexing in his cheek. "I work clean-up patrol for my father the risk-taker in our business, and the job doesn't leave any room for error. My father makes as many enemies as he does friends in his line of work and it's not always easy smoothing over the rough edges he leaves behind."

Adam studied a bust of Athena along with a dark vase reproduction used to reward victorious Olympic athletes.

Something bothered her about his admission. Did he think she was like his father?

"You know you do not have to play diplomat this week." Seeing his brow furrow made her want to smooth it out with her fingertips as well as her words.

"No?"

"No," she said firmly, wishing they could start their day over again. "Since I do not know how to monitor my words most of the time, it would be very appealing if you were to say whatever you think, too."

She studied the Bast statue once more and took heart from seeing the warrior cat. In fact, the piece made her wonder if there was room in her Arabian Nights collection for a scent inspired by the image of female strength.

"You want the uncut, uncensored version of me?"

A thrill chased its way up her spine.

"Yes."

"Then why don't you consider coming somewhere a lot more private with me?"

The thrills splintered and multiplied.

"Are your uncensored words so wicked?"

"It's not my words that I'm concerned about keeping private." He grinned and her heart gave a little flip. "It's my uncensored actions that might be best kept between the two of us."

CHAPTER FIVE

ADAM WOULDN'T GIVE Danielle a chance to change her mind.

Not that she'd fully agreed to his plan anyhow. But she'd left the library with him, turning on her heel and stalking toward the door after his suggestion that he wanted to touch her.

Taste her.

He followed her now, past Caesar's Forum casino and an espresso bar toward the elevators. She made a sharp turn before she reached them, pushing through a door to an open deck facing away from Corfu. He hurried to hold the door for her, realizing she'd cleverly chosen the quiet side of the ship. Unused shuffleboard courts sat beneath rows of lifeboats. It wasn't the most scenic of *Alexandra's Dream*'s decks, but the element of privacy made it perfect for what he had in mind.

"I like your taste in private spaces." Adam followed her to the end of the rail, where the polished mahogany bar met a wall with a "staff only" door.

"I feel a little guilty for keeping you on board

when Greece awaits us on the other side of the ship." She reached up to tug a pin from her hair and the silky mass tumbled about her shoulders, tossed gently by the sea breeze drifting in off the water.

"The only thing I'm interested in is still on board." He studied her carefully, looking for cues she wanted the same things he did as she tucked the hairpin inside a tiny purse.

The strapless dress she wore clung to her curves through a miracle of nature, held together with nothing but a zipper snaking up one side. He was all too aware of how easily it could slide right off her slender body.

His fingers itched to touch the fabric to see if he was right.

"Sometimes our true interests come as a surprise to us, don't they?" Her accent was the sexiest sound he'd ever heard.

She watched him closely, and he had the distinct impression that she'd surprised herself by agreeing to be alone with him. He would make sure she didn't change her mind. He hadn't expected such a sophisticated, worldly woman to be nervous.

"I can tell you where your interests lie." He reached for her fingers where they rested on the rail. "Give me your hand."

Her gaze narrowed but she obliged him.

"I hardly know myself most days. I do not think—"

"You would know yourself better if you'd ever

had your palm read before." He wasn't above dusting off an old parlor trick as an excuse to touch her.

"You're kidding." She fisted her right hand, hiding it from him while he held it fast.

"No, I'm not kidding." Gently, he pried her fingers open again. "I had a Czechoslovakian nanny for a few years and she taught me all about the fine art of palm reading."

Marenka had been a grounding force in his life during the years his mother had been sick and his father had started to lose himself in his business. The time he'd spent with Marenka had been the least harried of his life. The rest had been a roller coaster.

Hell, most days he was convinced he still rode that same damn amusement park ride but without the thrill—until he met Danielle.

"Do not tell me my professional future," Danielle warned, bending her head with his to study her palm. "I do not want you to jinx my ability to promote Les Rêves to Ahmed this week and, yes, I am a bit superstitious."

He smoothed a finger down the center of her palm and familiarized himself with the shape of her.

"Done. Mum's the word on your company's future." Not that he even remembered where the lines for financial success were located. He struggled to recall what Marenka had taught him. "This is your dominant hand, correct?" He hadn't seen her write, but she seemed to use her right hand more than her left.

"Yes. Unless my life looks better on this hand." She scrutinized her left palm and compared it briefly to the one he studied.

"I think we're safe with this one." He struggled to focus on his reading. What he really wanted to do was to place her hand on his chest and then wrap her in his arms. "You have long fingers and a cone-shaped hand which suggest you are an artist at heart."

"Are you making that up?"

She sounded serious. Concerned.

"A lot of palm reading is in the interpretation, but according to Marenka, those are signs of creativity. She said my square palm indicated a life of hard work and less creativity."

"But you're independently wealthy." Skepticism permeated her words. "Have you worked hard?"

"Up until yesterday, I worked every day including weekends for six straight weeks to maintain the business dealings I had in motion and to convince my father not to purchase a radio station one week and a newspaper chain the next. Believe me, the palm reading was true for me."

"I only questioned you because my mother was an artist and following in her footsteps has always been a dream of mine."

He filed that bit of information away.

"But your creativity might be channeled into your current business. You seem to love perfume making."

Nodding, she peered back down at their joined hands.

"What else does it say?"

"There is a separation between your heart line and your head line, which indicates you are not as impulsive as you believe yourself to be." He traced those distinct lines, feeling her pulse throbbing gently beneath her soft skin.

"I will have to tell my brother—Marcel—that he has been wrong about me all these years." She lifted her head to smile up at him, so close he could have kissed her.

And he wanted to kiss her.

They stood silently for a long moment, each taking the other's measure in the warm afternoon sunlight.

"How does my love life look to you?" Her voice was a breathy whisper that teased his senses.

"I happen to know it's getting better by the second," he confided, his thumb tracing a circle around the center of her palm.

Her eyelids fluttered in response and he closed the space between them to capture her lush mouth. Her lips parted with speed quickness and he deepened the kiss.

She shivered lightly against him and he tugged her hand free to place her palm on his chest before he folded her in his arms. Her head tipped back in silent surrender, and hot sensation flooded through him as her body pressed against his.

He'd dreamed of this the night before, imagining exactly what she'd feel like if he ever had the chance to hold her. The reality was even better than those heated imaginings, her sweet sighs an enticing sound that worked some kind of dark, sensual magic on him. The need to steal her away some place remote was too strong to ignore. He wanted to lay her down. To cover her body with his....

"Danielle." He pulled back sharply while he still could. "Let me walk you back to your room."

"I—" She shook her head, her expression confused. Wary. "I can't think. I don't know."

Her refusal was logical. Sensible. And...ah hell, he needed to have some space between them before he forgot everything else but kissing her again.

"I have meetings tomorrow, but why don't we go ashore in Naples together the next day? We can hire a boat to take us out to Capri." He wouldn't be able to sleep tonight if he didn't know he could spend time with her again. "I'll meet you at your stateroom at noon. Okay?"

He held his breath, unable to breathe in the same air as her without wanting to keep kissing her.

"*Oui.*" She nodded, her violet eyes a narrow rim around dilated pupils. "Until then."

She refused his offer to walk her back to her room, which was probably wise considering how much he wanted to cross that threshold when they got there. He let her go, hoping she would trust him a little more each day, because he didn't know how he would hold himself back the next time he kissed her that way. He'd dated enough women to know that chemistry like theirs didn't come along often. And since tomorrow would be the third day of the cruise, they only had so much time left to explore the heat that simmered between them.

THE SHIP'S newest destination tempted her.

The Maltese Islands beckoned to her every time she looked out over the ship's rail, but Danielle attended the fragrance exhibition and two meetings the next morning in the hope of running into the Dubai-based retailer again. She preferred socializing outside their formally scheduled meetings wherever possible. Adam was working today, too, and the knowledge spurred her to be all the more industrious about pursuing business over pleasure.

Still, there had been no sign of Ahmed Ramnathan, the quiet and studious-looking businessman who'd been so receptive of her pitch for Les Rêves's new Arabian Nights line. A Parisian perfumer told Danielle he thought Ahmed had attended a conference-sponsored tour of Valletta to see St. John's Co-Cathedral. It boasted an extensive collection of Flemish tapestries and—if Danielle's memory served—a Caravaggio that her mother had seen once. Danielle wished now she had taken the tour.

Leaving the last of her meetings behind, she took a set of stairs to deck ten in an effort to burn off a few extra calories from the fantastic food served on the ship. Apparently the head chef was new to *Alexandra's Dream*, but Danielle had read about his culinary exploits before, since he used to have a successful restaurant just down the French coast from her. Everything about the cruise seemed decadent and delightful, although she had noticed the bath products in her stateroom weren't top of the line. She'd made a mental note to seek out the cruise line's purchasing agent when she returned home to see if she could work up a deal to have some of Les Rêves's new soaps and lotions on board instead.

She had almost reached her destination when she spotted a familiar figure on his way down the stairs.

"Father Connelly?" She paused to address the priest who'd given the lecture on classical antiquities.

"I don't believe I've had the pleasure." The priest, a gray-haired, robust-looking man in his fifties, extended his hand.

His companion, an officer with two and a half stripes, nodded briefly to her before continuing down the stairs.

"I'm Danielle Chevalier, Father." She shook his hand and found herself tugged into the corner of the staircase landing. "I attended your cocktail party and part of your lecture yesterday."

"Ah, yes!" He snapped his fingers in recognition. "You stood in the back while I was speaking."

An older woman descended past them and Father Connelly winked at her, eliciting a blush. Apparently the priestly calling hadn't dimmed his love of flirting.

"I wanted to ask you about the Bast statue in the ship's collection." She was already designing perfume bottles and potential scent combinations inspired by the piece.

"You plan to test the poor clergyman when his notes are nowhere in sight?" he teased, patting his pockets as if searching for a lost notebook. "You are a cruel woman, Ms. Chevalier."

"I don't need to know anything specific," she assured him. "But I am curious about the goddess in general and I thought you might be able to tell me more than what you included in the lecture."

Perhaps she'd been attracted to Bast because of the lack of warrior-like qualities in herself. The longer she thought about Marcel's phone call and his insistence she stay away from Adam, the more certain she became that she had not fought hard enough for independence and respect from her family.

What woman couldn't use a little warrior spirit in her life?

"Bless you for taking it easy on me." He smiled. "Bast, or Bastet, is the daughter of the Egyptian sun god Re. And, like most ancient deity figures, the more you read about her, the more conflicting the information. But she is supposed to be the embodiment of the rage in Re's eye, and she is a goddess of both household protection and vengeance. Her domain is as far-reaching as the stories about her powers and her importance."

He went on to describe mummified cats found throughout the same region as the statue, and shared a few other facts that weren't relevant to her plans for a new perfume inspired by the figure. When he seemed to have exhausted his knowledge on the subject, she shook his hand and left to find her stateroom.

There would be gardens to visit in Capri tomorrow, and she wanted to be sure her nose was ready to seek out the raw fragrances she needed to mix a perfume that would inspire a woman's strength as well as her femininity. She could hardly wait to get to work.

If only finding her own strength were as simple as developing a new scent.

"WHAT THE HELL do you think you're doing?" Giorgio Tzekas, the ship's first officer, was pissed off at him again.

Mike O'Connor, who went by Father Patrick Connelly on the ship, was beginning to think his sideline as Giorgio's therapist would overshadow their real mission on board *Alexandra's Dream*. The guy was seriously unstable.

"What?" Mike feigned cluelessness. The two men were in Giorgio's stateroom. "I can't have a conversation with a beautiful woman? Ms. Chevalier is worth any man's time."

Giorgio paced his way over to the peephole and peered out into the ship's corridor. "Will you keep your voice down? And you know damn good and well that I mean what the hell are you doing mixing genuine artifacts from my expeditions with the reproductions displayed in the library?"

Mike knew that bit of cleverness wouldn't go overlooked for long. Too bad Giorgio didn't have a creative mind when it came to perfecting the art of the scam. But then, that's the way it was with people who kept one foot in the law-abiding world and one foot on the dark side. They were constantly worried their worlds would collide.

Smooth, eloquent lies. That's what was needed in their current scheme to smuggle priceless artifacts from the Mediterranean into the United States after the ship's reposition cruise.

The boss demanded perfection and Mike enjoyed that challenge. He admired the way the operation was being run so far, even if he'd never met the boss other than a few furtive phone calls to exchange information. Mike couldn't wait to see how the artifacts were going to be smuggled off the ship. For now, he didn't think that would be his department. It was tough enough getting things on board.

"A brilliant idea, isn't it?" Mike helped himself to a drink from Giorgio's minibar selection. The officer's room was ten times nicer than the stateroom Mike had been offered as part of his lecturer gig. At least he didn't have to share it the way the lower-level crew members did. Some of them had to bunk with six people in a room.

When Giorgio didn't respond, Mike figured he needed to spell out the benefits of the plan.

"This way we don't have to worry about hiding anything or getting caught with suspicious goods after those last few artifacts were discovered in the potted plants—your idea, you might recall. Now everything is out in the open and passed off as reproductions. As I pick up new things, we'll add them to the collection as fakes."

Giorgio glared at him.

"Brilliant is not what I would have called it. There has been more attention on your collection ever since those pieces were discovered. And the cleaning staff is grumbling about having to dust all those breakables."

"Remind me why I care what the guy with the mop thinks?" Mike poured himself a second drink since the bartender in the cigar club was convinced a priest shouldn't receive full-strength alcohol.

Giorgio swore. Or so Mike supposed. The words he rattled off in Greek didn't exactly sound complimentary.

"A pissed-off guy with a mop is more likely to bring attention to your display from crew and passengers alike. A cruise liner like this is a rumor mill. Someone starts talking, and pretty soon it's the conversational topic for the whole ship. Nick Pappas is looking for any reason at all to link me to trouble. I guarantee you the boss isn't going to like all that attention."

"Don't worry about Captain Pappas. And I guarantee the boss won't appreciate having a pussy on staff. Will you relax?" Mike thought about asking Danielle Chevalier out for a drink to discuss Bast in more detail. Single women were all over the ship and there was no way he could ignore that fact for the whole season.

Tuning out whatever Giorgio was saying now, Mike set down his glass abruptly.

"I'm out of here." It would be easy to find out which room Danielle was in since the woman at the purser's desk liked him. Perhaps he'd see if Danielle wanted to explore one of the ports with him this week to provide a much needed distraction.

"Don't forget you have to meet our contact tomorrow to pick up new pieces." Giorgio hovered over him like an old woman as he made his way toward the door.

"I'm going to score tomorrow." Shaking off Giorgio's tense words, Mike stepped out into the corridor. "You can count on it."

CHAPTER SIX

"IS EVERYTHING ALL right back home?" Adam asked Danielle the next day as he rowed their boat through the water that would lead them to *La Grotta Azzura*, Capri's famous blue grotto.

She'd been quiet ever since returning from a phone call she'd had to her brother shortly after they'd arrived in Anacapri, a section of Capri that was so lush and beautiful he regretted not traveling more before now.

Blue water surrounded them now as the hills of the island shrank slightly in the distance. Three other small boats rowed near them and larger vessels with tour groups drifted ahead and behind them, waiting to enter the grotto. Dozens of cruise passengers had chosen to tour Capri during the ship's stay in Naples. Apparently the grotto was a major attraction even though Adam had never heard of it. Something about cruising the Mediterranean this week made him think he'd been living in too isolated a world. He knew he'd been busting his butt with work for years, but not until this trip had he realized he was also living with his head under a rock.

"I am unsure." Danielle shook her head as if trying to shake off a dark mood. "My brother didn't say anything was wrong, but his voice—Marcel did not sound like himself. He even neglected to ask me about you, and I know for a fact he is worried about you and I seeing each other."

Adam leaned forward to dip the oars behind him and then pulled back hard, taking pleasure from the way the simple, clear-cut task propelled them through the water faster. There was something reassuring about being able to control an end result by how hard you worked to achieve it. Too often in business that wasn't the case.

"What is there to worry about?" He pulled the oars out of the water, pausing to let them drip.

"I have…how shall we say? A poor track record when it comes to men." She repositioned her legs to one side of the boat, her tanned shapely calves catching his eye.

As always, she looked phenomenal in linen shorts and jacket, every inch the wealthy European businesswoman. Her narrow leather belt and small designer satchel probably cost as much as his whole outfit. A silk tank top hugged her curves beneath the jacket, the delicate white fabric allowing him tantalizing glimpses of some kind of lace thing underneath.

"*You* have a poor track record? I find that hard to believe." Any man would want to claim a woman like Danielle for his own.

She propped a pair of big sunglasses on her head, revealing her eyes.

"The last man I grew attached to stole a valuable perfume formula before I went to market with the product."

"Bastard." He wondered what had been more devastating for her—the knock to her business or the toll it must have taken on her heart.

Not to mention her pride.

"Precisely." She peered around to see a small boat with tourists float into the grotto under a low rock wall.

"But one jerk doesn't make a bad track record. Everyone has lousy luck in romance now and then. Witness my relationship with Jessica, which she completely manipulated." He turned around to judge the distance to the grotto. The man who'd rented them the boat told him to make sure they lay down as they went under the low-hanging cave wall since an unexpected wave could lift the craft high enough to risk injury.

"Ah, but he was just one example." She waved another boat ahead of them as he backed near the entrance. The couple near them shouted something that sounded like Italian for thank you.

"I hope he's the worst case." The guy had a hell of a nerve to hurt her on both a personal and professional level.

"He is," Danielle acknowledged. "The others just dated me for the wealth of my mother's estate. My brother Marcel calls them lazy pretty boys."

"Then Marcel ought to think I'm all aces since I haven't taken a day off in six weeks or a week off in six years." He propped the oars up again so they could settle themselves inside the boat before they floated under the entrance wall. "And no one's ever accused me of being a pretty boy."

He scowled at the very idea.

"No?" She smiled, sliding to one side of her seat. "Do you really think your Hollywood princess would wish to be photographed with an unattractive man?"

"Hell, yeah. It makes her look better." He wished they hadn't been talking about another woman at the very moment they needed to lie down together, possibly his only chance to get horizontal with her today.

He put his feet up on her seat while she stretched out beside him, their bodies spanning the two metal seats like bridges. He slipped his arm around her, cushioning her head and shoulders.

"Your track record is about to improve," he assured her, speaking into her ear through the veil of her hair.

The boat floated slowly beneath the rock wall, the light, the air and the sounds around them changing as they entered the grotto. The place smelled earthy and damp without the benefit of a fresh breeze.

"Oh." Danielle's breath caught as the flood of intense blue light washed over them.

"Wow." Adam didn't sit up even, though they'd

cleared the low wall to float freely inside the grotto by now. The experience of holding Danielle, her head resting on his shoulder, seemed even more amazing than the indigo spectacle drenching their bodies in rich color.

"It's like we fell into the sky." Danielle's voice remained hushed, her quiet no doubt inspired by the same awe that kept the other boaters calm, too.

The boating parties that had been loud and raucous and multilingual outside the cave now shared a universal silence as they took in a sight that seemed almost sacred.

The space was no bigger than a half a football field, the rocks above them echoing back the liquid sounds of waves lapping at the sides of the boats.

"Let's look at the water," Adam said finally, reluctant to move but not wanting Danielle to miss out on the full experience of the grotto.

Her cheek grazed his chest for an instant before she righted herself, her long, dark hair sliding down his body like a lover's fingers.

"C'est magnifique." She dipped her hand in the water, which was colored as richly as the air, and it took on an ultraviolet hue.

"Too bad they don't let people swim in here." He leaned behind her to immerse his hand in the water next to hers.

"We have found a magical place, no?" She turned to smile at him over her shoulder and he felt the air sucked right out of his lungs. Twisting in her seat to face him, she trailed her wet hand up his arm, coating his skin with fine blue mist.

His reaction was swift and fierce as heat flared deep inside him.

"Anyone ever tell you that you have a very sensuous nature?" He shook his head. "Does that sound like the world's worst pick-up line?"

Her fingers trailed down to the water again and back up his arm, technically cooling his skin but somehow making his blood simmer at the same time. He wanted to sink down into the bottom of the boat with her and never come up.

"It is no pick-up line when it is true. We are only half living if we do not use all our senses to appreciate life."

Their boat might have been floating straight into a rock wall and Adam would never have known it. He seemed to be drowning in a blue sea of longing.

He gripped her hand at the top of his shoulder and held her fast, twining their fingers as he folded her palm into his own.

"I'm feeling very appreciative right now." He breathed in the scent of her mingled with damp rock and salt water. "If you let me taste you, I'll show you how much."

Her eyes lingered on his mouth before she licked her lips. That was all the answer he needed.

He tipped her head back, angling her beneath him before he lowered his mouth to hers. A soft sigh escaped her, tempting him to pull her to the floor of the boat again where they might be hidden from view.

Just for a moment.

They sank together, as if drawn by her will as much as his, their boat floating listlessly around the cavern. Untwining their hands, he skimmed her jacket off her shoulders as he eased her down onto the worn wool throw that had been given to them with the boat for the afternoon. The scent of her skin incited a hot, possessive reaction, and Adam knew that even if he never recognized the low notes or the high notes in the fragrance, he would be turned on by it for the rest of his life.

The blue light made her pale skin almost transparent and she glowed beneath his touch as he ran one fingertip along the strap of her silk tank top. It drooped off her shoulder, and her back arched.

The sounds of their breathing filled his ears, the splashing boats and soft murmurs of tourists fading away as he bent his head to sample the delicate column of her throat.

Danielle might have been able to resist his touch, but Adam's lips silenced any thought she might have had to keep their relationship more private. This man's lips could persuade her to do anything, and she seriously feared she would start peeling off her clothes with no more encouragement than the swirl of his tongue in the hollow at the base of her throat.

She lay there mesmerized by the blue of the grotto and the heat of Adam's passion, powerless to do anything but follow the wanton urging of her long-denied body.

His mouth descended lower and she thought she would expire with want. She trembled in dark anticipation of his mouth on her breast, even knowing they needed to put an end to their sweet explorations for propriety's sake.

But no one could see them, a little voice inside her argued, her shoulders shrugging in the hope she might wriggle more of herself out of the silk tank top she wore. Liquid heat pooled in her belly.

"I want to be alone with you." Adam's quiet words drummed into her brain along with distant hints of returning reason. "I owe you so much better than this."

They stared at one another, hearts racing as if they'd run a marathon, and she marveled that she could have as strong an effect on him as he had on her.

"I don't want to rush and yet I can't help rushing." Danielle hadn't acknowledged that before, but she had to admit that perhaps she'd been partly to blame for allowing her sensual nature to dictate decisions in the past. "Perhaps that is the downside to being impetuous."

"There is no downside." He lifted himself to peer over the edge of the boat before he straightened her drooping tank top and drew her upright to sit beside him again. "I wish I could be more like you."

His words found root in her heart, even if she knew he couldn't possibly mean them.

"That is the kisses talking," she chided him, drawing her linen jacket around her shoulders in a weak effort to stamp out the memory of Adam's lips on her skin.

"No." He moved the oars from their locked position and dipped them down into the blue water. "That is the experience of a cynic who spends months on end buried in business deals and acting as negotiator for a bunch of overeducated know-it-alls who never learned how to play well with others. Half the people I work with don't know there's more to life than making the almighty dollar. And to tell you the truth, I don't think I realized it myself until three days ago."

The smooth efficiency with which he rowed them through the water made her think maybe he wasn't exaggerating. Did Adam normally live and breathe business? He could certainly adopt a facade of detached competency when he wished, like now with the boat. Or when he assured her he didn't mind the competition for the Dubai retail account. Had he seemed so confident because of a driven nature that didn't allow him to fail?

"Get down," he ordered, lining up the boat with the entrance of the grotto so they could leave the cave.

She hunkered down again, but the warmth of all they'd shared was tinged with her fear that once again she'd allowed herself to get close to a man she didn't understand.

Because as much as she was attracted to Adam, she couldn't afford to let those emotions derail her from the bargain they'd made. They could pursue a relationship on board *Alexandra's Dream*, but once they returned home, she'd have to put him in her past.

She was already beginning to think she'd set herself up for an impossible task.

ALONE TIME was in short supply on a Mediterranean cruise ship, Adam admitted to himself the next day as he dressed for a luncheon sponsored by the perfume association as one of the conference events.

The stolen moments in the bottom of a row boat with Danielle were as close as he'd come to being alone with her. The way he wanted.

But that would change today. The ship docked in Civitavecchia this morning and would spend a full day into late evening there so that passengers could have more time to make the trek inland to Rome. Adam had reserved a car near the pier in case he could talk Danielle into spending some time on shore with him after the luncheon. Alone.

The phone rang on his way out the door as he juggled a fresh gardenia in one hand, the receiver in the other.

"Hello?"

"It's Joe. Got any news for me?" His brother's voice came over the line loud and strong, even with music blaring in the background. Joe had missed the hard rock era while it was happening, but he took great pleasure in dredging it up with vintage vinyl on a record player he kept in his office.

"Yeah I got news. AC-DC is playing too damn loud." He held the phone away from his ear until the decibel level sank.

"Sorry. But what's going on with the Dubai retailer? I've been staring at my fax machine waiting for you to send some contracts." Joe still drummed the beat on his desk with a pencil. Adam didn't need a visual. Joe had been turning everyday household items into drumsticks from the time he was two.

"No deal yet, but I'm only just warming up and finding my way around the perfume world. I figured it didn't make much sense to make my pitch before I picked up the lingo." His words made him remember Danielle's loser boyfriend who'd stolen her perfume recipe, and he vowed not to ask her any more about fragrance-making. He'd be damned if he would give her any reason to compare him to relationships she'd had in the past. If he needed to know anything else about perfumes, he'd ask someone from another company.

"Really?" Joe's drumming stopped. "That sounds downright prudent of you, bro. I'm feeling guilty now that I took a bet against you in the office pool."

"You've got to be kidding me." Adam knew the support staff at Burns Inc. were as addicted to inter-office betting as his brother and father, but he refused to think Joe would throw his money away by betting against Adam. "Why would you think I'd mess this up when it's the one and only goal you set for me the entire cruise? I've researched the hell out of this Dubai rep. I know what he'll want to see from us. I shot pool with him last night just to shoot the breeze and get inside the guy's head. Shit, Joe, I probably close five business deals a month."

Joe's short bark of laughter pissed him off.

"But you play to your strengths at home by managing business within your frame of reference. Besides, the way you bitched and moaned about taking this cruise and spending the week with a bunch of fragrance nuts, I just figured—"

"You figured wrong." Adam's grip tightened on the gardenia and he wanted the hell out of this conversation. "What am I, the weak link in the company and I never knew it?"

"Hell, no. What's the matter with you? We were just amused at the idea of Joe Jock courting the European jet-setters and were having a good time spinning scenarios for how that might be working out."

Adam stared out his balcony doors at the port city of Civitavecchia on the far side of the pier and tried to relax, knowing he was probably uptight at the possibility he really couldn't relate to these people. To Danielle.

And yeah, for this week at least, he wanted to be a part of her world.

"It's working out fine. I'm just here wondering why I didn't take a vacation sooner."

"What kind of sacrilege are they teaching you over there?" Joe's drumming picked up again, slower now. "That's the most anti-Burns statement I've ever heard you make."

"How long are we supposed to live for work?" He didn't have time to get into all the revelations that had bombarded him this week, but he couldn't help toss out that one key question. "You know, we've been to Rome multiple times on business with Dad and I don't think I've ever seen any of it outside hotel conference centers and the occasional workout room."

There was something seriously screwed up about that.

"And now you've got a hankering to see the Eternal City?"

"More like a rebel need to have a life." Was that so freaking surprising? "I'm gonna be late for a meeting, Joe, but I'll give you a call when I clinch the deal."

"Okay, but—"

"And don't ever bet against your blood, man. Big mistake." He hung up the phone and left his suite, more than ready to see Danielle and forget about business breathing down his neck.

It was the only time Adam could ever remember wanting to walk away from a competition. He wouldn't, of course. But damn it, this was one game he wasn't looking forward to winning.

CHAPTER SEVEN

"DO YOU WANT to know what the French papers have to say about you, Adam?" Danielle spun beneath his arm as they danced across the wooden floor of the Polaris Lounge during the perfumers' luncheon reception. Dancing might be unusual for a traditional lunch gathering, but part of the entertainment for the event was dance lessons from six of the ship's dancers, and Danielle had to admit it was fun to have an excuse to be in Adam's arms.

The furniture had been moved to the side of the room for the afternoon's event, the walls draped with silver silk, the same shade as a new perfume bottle its manufacturer was spending big bucks to promote. Danielle admired the spread even as she wondered how she'd ever compete when it came time to bring her new Arabian Nights line to market.

Sure she had ideas. But financing them…that was always the tough part. With any luck, the Dubai retailer would be so enthused about the new products that they'd put some money behind the effort to promote them.

Adam's timing was impeccable, his feet easily picking up the rhythm of their dance—a basso dance. Could she help it if her brain chose that moment to recall the age-old adage about men who were good at dancing? Of course, it stood to reason that men who would take the time to learn physical moves that pleased a woman would also…

Her cheeks flushed at the sudden vivid image that rose to her mind, her body keenly aware of his body as his hand rested on her strapless purple sheath dress. She'd removed the matching shrug that went with the dress when it came time to dance.

"Uh, oh. What exactly did the papers say? It can't be so bad it makes you blush." Adam released her hand to tip her chin up and study her face.

"No," she denied quickly, forcing her thoughts back to her latest conversation with Marcel, in which he'd reiterated his plea to sell off the business while warning her away from Adam at the same time. "It isn't all that bad, considering your position with your company. You've probably heard most of the rumors already anyhow."

She took his hand in hers again, resuming their dance posture where the boundaries between them were fixed, even if they were…tantalizing.

"But they bother you?" He twirled her past an older couple who ran a small fragrance company outside Paris. Danielle remembered her mother once told her the pair could be seen all around the city every spring, holding hands and walking the streets like new lovers.

Danielle had never forgotten that story, her own wistful heart longing to find that kind of happiness.

"They don't bother me." She shrugged as she kept step with him, not sure how to explain her relationship with her stern brother. "But they bother Marcel, and that will cause me a bit of grief this week until I can return home with my heart unscathed and my perfume recipes still a secret. I guess I have not learned how to shut him out of my private life when our business worlds are so intertwined."

The band finished the tune, and Adam and Danielle clapped their appreciation. Her hip remained warm from his touch even though he had released her. As the band started a lively salsa, Adam gestured toward the exit and she nodded, ready for a little air after the dancing and the time spent making small talk with business associates. Dancing with Adam had been her only chance to let her guard down since she'd arrived. She signaled him to wait as she retrieved her shrug and handbag.

"Earlier today I would have told you my brother and I have a great working relationship," Adam said as they headed out to the deck. The scents of the afternoon air rode the breeze and lifted Danielle's hair from her warm neck, refreshing her skin and her spirits.

"But not now?" she asked, curious about Adam's family.

"I never thought the day would come when I would say my brother was more driven than me, but after talking to him on the phone I realized he is. I might be quicker to make work a competition, but even though Joe is quieter about his commitment to the business, he has a fierce streak in him that demands the company succeed."

"Does that bother you?" She wasn't sure what to make of his subdued tone. "I know it can be difficult for a family to be in business together."

A bar was set up on the outdoor deck and a smattering of people were taking in the fresh air. Paper lanterns had been strung overhead, creating a party atmosphere, even though they hadn't been lit yet. From this distance, the sound of music from the Civitavecchia port drifted on the air, the water amplifying the sounds between the ship and the shore.

"It doesn't bother me. But it makes me realize he's going to have plans for the company after our father retires, even if he's been downplaying his interest in the top spot." He nodded to one of the officers strolling through the party before he turned to look out over the water.

Danielle admired how quickly he'd made friends on board, a testament to his warm nature and interest in others. She liked that about Adam.

"Did you hope to take charge once your father leaves?" She knew that kind of promotion would mean she'd never see him again even professionally. The CEO of Burns Inc. wouldn't spend his time wooing accounts for one of his companies, even if Prestige Scents continued to be one of the biggest assets in the family empire.

"No." Adam's answer was quick. Resolute. "I've had all I can handle the last few years. I'd like to work less as I get older. Not more."

His hand trailed down her shoulder, his finger dipping lightly into the curve of her elbow.

"So your brother's quiet ambition should come as good news." She failed to understand Adam's brooding mood.

"It should," he agreed, skimming her tender flesh in a lazy circle. "I just don't know what to make of surprises sometimes, and this…hell, this caught me by surprise."

She couldn't hold back a shiver at the exquisite feel of his touch.

A new song began in the Polaris Lounge, drowning out the sounds from the Civitavecchia port. The lively music lifted her spirits, reminding her she had a rare and magical window of time with Adam before she had to relinquish her sexy American to whatever his future might hold.

"Maybe we should not think about any of this today." Seized with the mischievous mood that occasionally got her into trouble, she tried to remember the last time she'd gotten to walk around the streets of Italy. "Maybe I should forget that I have been cast under a romantic spell by a powerful American businessman the tabloids call New York's most eligible player."

He rolled his eyes. "Hey, wait a minute."

She pressed her finger to his lips, enjoying the feel of him.

"Perhaps you should forget that your brother is about to climb over your strong shoulders to seize your father's company. And neither of us should think about all we have riding on the Dubai retailer. Maybe we ought to just forget all of it and go take Civitavecchia—or even Rome—by storm."

"A couple of cruise ship pirates?" His blue gaze went from her to the shoreline and back again.

"We'll drink in the taverns and…" She hesitated but still couldn't stop herself from saying what else she wanted. "And we'll let our passions run wild after the great restraint we've shown at sea."

Adam grinned but his eyes took on a heated light that shot a thrill clear to her toes.

"You mean, I'm finally going to see the bold and brazen side of Danielle Chevalier that I've heard so much about?"

"Do you have your boarding pass with you?"

He felt his jacket pocket.

"Yes."

"Then you can meet my wild alter ego. But only if you can catch her."

Spinning on her heel, she darted through the crowd toward the exit, her heart thumping with excitement to have fun and play. To flirt and be flirted with.

God, she'd missed this.

Laughing her joy, she turned to look over her shoulder as she bolted down a staircase and saw

Adam close on her heels, his expression not quite as teasing as hers.

Utter determination was etched in his features and Danielle could hardly wait to see where the day—and the night that followed—would lead.

No DOUBT ABOUT IT, Danielle was different today.

He'd chased her off the boat and down the pier, but she'd managed to elude his grip whenever he got close. Then again, he didn't mind giving her room to play her game since he could tell by her eyes they would be spending this night together.

The realization tantalized him as much as her decision to ditch the perfumers' luncheon in favor of spending time alone together. After his pool game with Ahmed, Adam felt all the more certain of the guy's willingness to work with Prestige Scents. Adam didn't need to schmooze his way through the shipside party to feel like he'd done his job today.

"Are you coming?" she called over her shoulder as she neared the street where shuttles and taxis awaited cruise passengers who wanted to make the ninety-minute trip into Rome. He hoped the car ride wouldn't dampen her spirit, but he looked forward to some time alone with her after the demands on her schedule the past two days.

"Lady, you couldn't lose me if you tried." He caught up to her finally, steering her away from the public taxis to a car he'd called earlier in the day.

"You planned to come into Rome?" she asked, voice lightly accusing.

"No. But I've been hoping." He nodded to the driver and tried not to notice Danielle's enticing rear view as she climbed into the limousine.

"A prepared man." He stepped into the car and took a seat beside her on crushed red velvet that had seen better days. "I can admire that."

"Excellent. After having your brother give you an earful about my sordid past, it's a relief to know you can still find things to appreciate about me." He settled back in the seat as the car took off, the chauffeur leaving the privacy window closed and a bottle of local Italian wine chilling in a special compartment to Adam's right.

Just as he'd requested.

And after the day of jarring personal and professional revelations he'd had, Adam appreciated the simple pleasure of having his demands met.

"It wasn't entirely sordid." She arched a delicate eyebrow at him. "He e-mailed me a few of the articles and I found a delicious photo of you running on a beach in Nantucket in your swim trunks. All those flexing muscles—" she fanned her face "—they made quite an impression on me."

Shaking his head, he reached for the wine and removed the cork.

"I'd rather make the impression in person. Especially since I remember the kind of article that went along with that picture." He'd been labeled a playboy or an eligible bachelor, the kind of garbage that had led to his decision to play less of a public role in Burns Inc.

Of course, being chased around by a prominent actress had meant renewed media interest in his personal life the last six months. The added attention was the reason he'd begged Joe to take his place on the Jet Ski with Jessica. No doubt a photo of his brother hurtling over the Jet Ski could be found somewhere on the Internet for anyone inclined to hunt.

"That is why I thought you looked familiar when I first saw you," Danielle said. "I'd seen your face in the social pages of our papers before, I'm sure. European papers tend to follow royalty and money over the Hollywood celebrities that Americans are so fascinated with." Danielle took the glass of wine he handed her and clinked it lightly against his before stealing a sip. She closed her eyes in appreciation of the flavor and he couldn't tear his gaze away from her moist red lips and dark eyelashes.

And with one smart choice in vino, the limo driver just tripled his tip.

"Well, I don't know how I've ended up as a footnote in one column after another given I don't date that much." Adam felt compelled to point that out. Those stupid articles painted a much different picture of him. "But after Jessica decided to introduce me to the world of paparazzi, I seem to have become a favorite subject. Nothing close to what truly famous people have to contend with, obviously. But it's a strange experience."

"Your American starlet has been persistent and she obviously knows how to create her own small dramas for the cameras." Danielle held the wineglass up to the tinted window. Tilting the glass to the side, she seemed to assess the color. "She is smart to know how to work the system to her advantage."

"Smart?" Adam considered. "Opportunistic, maybe."

Danielle laughed and recrossed her legs. Her toe grazed his calf and he realized she'd removed her shoes.

"Let's not talk about Jessica." He set aside his wineglass, ready to be blunt with Danielle. "Let's talk about tonight."

"You know the paparazzi might catch up with you at any port, don't you?" Danielle's eyes were serious as she peered at him over the rim of her glass. "It's only a matter of time before the camera crew from Corfu tips off their tabloid journalist friends to your whereabouts."

"Let them come. At least when they take a photo of us together it will be an honest moment since you're more to me than a business acquaintance."

Danielle set her glass aside, too. Her long, dark hair draped over her shoulder with the movement, veiling parts of her from his sight.

He liked that about her—the way she could be sexy without saying a word. She exuded sexual confidence in other ways, too, by flirting with her eyes. The way she crossed her legs. Very hot.

"You flatter me, Adam. But we do not have to resign ourselves to media intrusion. Maybe we should give anyone within a camera a run for their money." The mischievous light returned to her eyes—the same one he'd seen on board the ship before she'd darted away from him.

"I forgot you're an Olympic runner in high heels." He reached down to run his hand lightly up her calf and was gratified to see her shiver.

"And Rome is a wonderful city to get lost in." She gestured vaguely with her fingers and then rested them on his tie.

"I'll be sure to let you lead the way." He lowered his voice as he homed in on her neck, needing a taste of her skin and a breath of her scent.

"All I need to know is where we are ultimately headed. Did you have a destination in mind? A café? One of the galleries?"

She arched into him as his mouth found the pulse throbbing just below the surface of her skin.

"I thought we'd stop off in the park at Villa Borghese. Maybe walk to the Trevi fountain and past the Coliseum. I've heard it's better to see a few things in Rome than to tackle too much."

"*Oui*. I have seen the park and it is beautiful." Her breath huffed faster, hands alighting on his shoulders as she hummed her satisfaction. "We will let our feet follow paths that are over two thousand years old. Who knows how many other lovers have chased each other through the Eternal City?"

He broke away, sitting up to look her in the eye.

"You're not trying to give me the slip the way you want to do to those photographers?"

The instep of her bare foot rubbed against his calf with slow deliberation and that wicked smile of hers unfurled.

"I am looking forward to being caught by you at the end of the night. Maybe sooner if we grow too restless on our trip into the city." Her fingers combed down the front of his jacket and it occurred to him that wearing a suit wasn't so bad when a woman like Danielle wanted to take you out of it. "That, I can promise."

Heat crawled all over his skin at her words, making him hope like hell the driver would floor it on the way back to the ship. He needed to get her alone, to peel away the exotic layers of this sexy French woman to find out what made her so different from other women.

She made him want to do things he'd never cared about before—making a crazy dash through Rome sound like foreplay. She'd convinced him that her conservative clothes were sexier than tight T-shirts and tiny cut-offs. She even made him want to find out more about perfume just so he could keep up with her.

He'd either lost his freaking mind or he was falling for her. Both possibilities scared the hell out of him. He'd seen what relationships could do to smart guys. The divorce rates of his friends were sky-high and his own long-term liasons had ended badly. For that matter, to call any of his relationships "long-term" would be a stretch at best with the work hours he kept.

But there sat Danielle, the most incredible woman he'd ever met, and he was ready to do whatever she wanted.

Hell.

He closed his eyes and found her lips. The sweet flavor of her kiss silenced all the warning bells going off in his brain, making her taste, her pleasure, the only important things right now. He kissed her for an endless moment, savoring the sweet satisfaction of that simple joining.

Her arms wound around his neck with no reservations, her breasts flattening against his chest, tantalizing him with images of what they could do until the car arrived in Rome.

Groaning with need, he hauled her up into his lap, seating her crossways so that her legs sprawled out along the seat beside him. Her hair draped down on either side of her face, curtaining their kiss and releasing the scent of fruity shampoo. He smoothed one side behind her shoulder, needing to see his hand on her body as he touched her.

"One question has been driving me crazy all week." He slipped his hand into the slit at the side of her dress, the fabric already parting to reveal toned calves tanned from their day on Capri.

"You wish to know the secret of my perfume success?" she teased, shifting in his lap so that her skirt slid farther up her legs.

"I'm sure my brother wishes I were that dedicated to work." He tugged her lower lip into his mouth and feasted for a long moment before he released it again. "I'm dying to know what kind of lingerie a sexy perfumer likes to wear."

"You naughty man," she chided, undoing the knot in his tie. "I believe you were thinking about my underwear when I was trying so hard to teach you about distinguishing scents."

"Maybe the desire to find out more about your panties made me want to be a better student. I think the incentive of getting you naked one day really helped my learning curve in the fragrance department." He fingered a sensitive spot behind her knee that made her breath catch.

"You are lying to me already and we've only known each other five days." She bent her knee farther, making her hem slide up until only the tops of her thighs remained covered by the purple silk. "And I was ready to believe you really needed my help."

"I do need you," he assured her, grateful for the tinted windows that gave them privacy despite the daylight. They'd entered the outskirts of Rome and foot traffic slowed the pace of the limo as it made its way along the narrow roads.

Danielle flexed her fingers against Adam's broad

chest, his words wrapping around her as seductively as his touch.

He needed her.

She knew the phrase might be just a general statement of physical desire, but to her it meant more. She felt the same need, and there was nothing remotely generic about it. Her thirst for Adam was far more than some random sexual itch. She longed for him at a deeper level, aching to connect with him, fearing she would fall apart if she didn't fulfill the need. Her fingers flew over his shirt buttons, her whole body reacting instinctively as she unveiled his bare chest to her touch.

"There is such vitality in American men," she observed to herself as much as him, marveling at the sinew and muscle beneath his heated flesh. "You accused me of having a sensuous nature, but I see this is where you indulge *your* physical side. You, *monsieur,* are an athlete."

She traced the lines that separated his abdominal muscles, the rock-hard plates lining up into six neat compartments. He closed his eyes and tipped his head back against the seat as she touched him, and it pleased her to know she could affect him that way.

"Work can be stressful." He reached out to imprison her fingers for a moment as he stared at her, his breathing shallow. "The gym is a good place to work off that stress in a socially acceptable way."

"Ah." She nodded her understanding and wriggled her fingers free again. "You need a release."

"Yes." He slipped his hands beneath her hair and pulled her to him.

She paused when they were nose-to-nose, breathing one another's air.

"I have an idea for a release you're going to like much more."

CHAPTER EIGHT

DANIELLE HADN'T REALIZED how much time had passed during those kisses until the driver's voice startled her right off Adam's lap.

"I can't take you any farther, sir, unless you would like me to take you to another park?"

She realized the limo had stopped as she tried to calm her unsteady heart. Her lips were swollen, her hair spilling untidily around her shoulders.

"Why?" Adam barked through the speaker. "Are we even close to the Villa Borghese?"

"Yes, but the road is closed off here by the *polizia* and I'm afraid it will not open for some time. It looks like there must have been trouble at the Galleria Borghese because all the streets around there have been closed."

Straightening her dress, Danielle peered out her window to orient herself.

"We can walk to the park from here. Or we can proceed straight to the Coliseum and see what we find along the way." She had been to the Villa de Borghese twice as a girl. Her mother loved to visit art galleries of all kinds, and believed the Italian masterpieces were the best in the world. Danielle didn't care where she and Adam went today as long as they spent time together.

After those heated moments in his lap, she looked forward to returning to the ship.

"How far is it?" Adam called to the driver, working on his shirt buttons. Outside, pedestrians walked past on the sidewalk near the closed street.

"A few blocks. No more." The driver launched into directions in broken English, but Danielle was already mapping the route in her mind.

"I know where it is," Danielle said. "Follow me."

She opened the car door on the side opposite him, not waiting for the driver to come around.

"Danielle, wait."

She heard Adam's voice behind her, but she wanted fresh air and a moment to steel herself before she fell into his arms again. She wasn't usually this bold with any man, but she'd been cautious for so long that something inside her seemed to rebel this week, clamoring for her to run wild.

Italian men were notorious flirts and they whistled their appreciation as she walked by. Unswayed by any man's attentions save Adam's, she shook out the shrug she'd discarded earlier and used it to protect her bare shoulders from the sun. The day had turned warm and humid, the city alive with scents of garlic and strong coffee, and a hint of the Tiber River nearby.

After he paid the driver, Adam caught up to her, his tie still undone around his neck. That note of disarray sent a thrill through her, reminding her that they would be shedding far more than his tie tonight.

When he reached her, he pulled her against him, his hands firm around her waist.

"I'm not letting you five feet from me in a strange city with packs of wolves prowling the streets." He eyed a pair of young men who edged past them, clearly not appreciating the extra attention she received.

The thought pleased her more than it should.

"You are jealous of strangers when only you get to take me home with you?" She couldn't resist reminding him what awaited them.

He muttered something under his breath, but she felt the vibration beneath her hands, resting on his chest.

"Until then, we're sightseeing, damn it." Turning her in his arms, he didn't chase her through the streets of Rome so much as propel her, and that turned out to be every bit as exciting.

The day was improving by the minute.

Hours later they returned to the ship and the privacy of Adam's suite. The car ride back to the port had required incredible restraint from both of them. All afternoon they'd savored the sights and sounds of Rome, but the pleasures of the Eternal City had almost lost out to the thrill of anticipation Danielle felt at the thought of being along with Adam tonight.

"Danielle." He spoke her name with a reverence

that made her knees weak as he locked the door behind them. His penthouse suite was more lavish than hers, and chills chased up her spine as she acknowledged she was completely in his hands tonight. The lights in the room were on a dim, soothing setting. Wine and fruit had been delivered to the room earlier and now sat on a cocktail table near a chaise longue. The ice in the ice bucket hadn't melted so much as a drop.

All day it had been that way. Adam had commanded attention and good service for them at the coffee shops, at the small galleries and with the deferential driver who'd driven them back to port even faster than on the outgoing trip.

"You live very well," she observed, feeling a little out of her league with this man for the first time since they had met.

Danielle had been so confident of herself, so certain her knowledge as a perfumer was superior to anything Adam might offer to win the Dubai account. But today she'd realized that Adam Burns was an extremely powerful man, and that intimidated her professionally even if it thrilled her on a more intimate level.

And—she reminded herself—tonight definitely wasn't about business.

"Yeah? Having you here with me makes me think you're right. I'm living very damn well tonight."

Compelled by the promise of his words and the heat in his eyes, Danielle closed the space between them and walked into his arms. Maybe it was the memories of their day in a romantic old city, but she could have sworn she heard violins swell triumphantly in her head.

Winding her arms around his neck, she arched up to kiss him and found herself swept off her feet. Adam cradled her to his chest, kissing her as he strode through the sitting area to the bedroom.

Danielle opened her eyes long enough to see a beautiful high bed draped in a white duvet. The covers had been turned back to show perfectly smooth sheets, the scent of starch mingling with lavender water as Adam laid her down.

"Lying here—it feels like sinking into heaven," she sighed on a contented breath, speaking more about Adam's presence around her than the luxurious sheets beneath her, but then, maybe he did not need to know that.

In fact, maybe he had not heard her, intent as he seemed now on lowering the zipper down the side of her dress. She arched up as he tugged the purple silk off her body, leaving her clad in only a strapless bra and undies.

"They match the color of your eyes." Adam grinned up at her wickedly as he wrenched his gaze from her panties. "Violet."

Only then did she recall his curiosity about her lingerie, an interest that had him tracing the silk over her hipbone. Making her shiver.

"There is no such thing as violet eyes," she disagreed, oddly pleased that her blunt-speaking American would spout this bit of romantic nonsense to her.

"Maybe I'm saying the wrong thing." He trailed a fingertip along her belly, skimming the line of her panties until she felt faint from the surge of heat that coursed through her. "Whatever color this is—" he dipped his finger ever so slightly beneath the waistband "—it's the same shade as your eyes."

No longer wishing to argue, Danielle couldn't even form words as his small movement produced delicious counter pressure on her most sensitive places. Her breath caught. Held. There was no room in her for air, her body so full of want she could not contain anything but this sharp need for Adam.

Fingers infused with that desire, she unfastened his shirt buttons and tugged away his crisp white dress shirt. She smoothed her fingers down his bare chest to his trousers.

His skin was on fire, burning with the same fever that seemed to grip her. She savored the solid strength of him, the hard muscle that forced her feminine softness to mold to him and around him. Even now, as he unfastened the front hook of her bra, her breasts flattened to accommodate the weight of him when he leaned down to kiss her.

"I've never been with someone so—soon." Her words caught as his thumb skated over one taut peak.

He stilled before pulling back to look her in the eye.

"Is it too fast for you? Tell me now and—"

She was already shaking her head. "No. It is not too fast. I just...well, I wanted you to know this is a first for me."

Adam heard Danielle's words, but it took a moment longer for them to reach his brain so he could process what they meant. She was giving him something special, something unique. Despite all her talk of a wild side, she'd never gone to bed with a man after knowing him for such a short period of time, and that meant—

Holy crap. He couldn't even think about what that meant right now while he held her almost-naked body against him, the scent of her skin making him drunk with want.

"I'm going to take such good care of you tonight you'll never regret it," he vowed, wishing he didn't have to cram a whole relationship into a ten-day cruise with this exotic woman. "I promise."

She wouldn't know he wasn't the kind of man to promise anything lightly. But he knew he was committing a hell of a lot with his words. He planned to make sure she went back to Nice a well-pleasured woman.

Unfastening his pants, he wrenched himself away long enough to stand and step out of his clothes. She looked like a goddess against the white sheets, her dark hair spilled over the pillowcase like one of the ship's classical statues come to life.

He spun her around to face him, her legs spilling off the bed. Stepping between her thighs, he strained toward her. Ready for her. He reached into the nightstand for the condom he'd placed there earlier and tore it open. He intended to keep her safe so they could enjoy this night to the fullest.

"You think of everything, I see." She ran her fingers up his thigh as he swept her panties down her endlessly long legs.

"I wanted everything perfect for you," he told her honestly. "I figured if I was ever lucky enough to get you here, I didn't want you to have to worry about a single thing."

She kissed her full lips to her finger and then reached up to place the kiss on his mouth. He stood over her, sheathed and ready. Oh, so ready.

Unable to wait any longer he leaned down and kissed her. She moaned, hips grinding against him until he positioned himself between her legs and edged his way inside.

Sweat broke out across his forehead as he tried to maintain control, but it wasn't easy with the sweet heat of her all around him, her legs wrapped around his waist to pull him closer. Tighter.

He felt himself losing control and he fought that sensation, needing to make this last for her. For them both.

"Danielle." He called out her name in a mixture of pleasure and anguish as she tilted her hips, making room to take every last inch of him.

"The fire inside is too great," she murmured brokenly, twisting beneath him. "It is like an unbearable fever. *Please*. I need you."

Her nails bit lightly into his hips as she reached for him and he knew all was lost. He thrust deeply inside her again and again, finding his rhythm. Or was it hers? He hardly knew where his needs ended and hers began in this wordless quest for fulfillment.

When she finally found that perfect high note to please her, she let out a keening cry he covered with his mouth, absorbing the uncensored sound of her pleasure as her body pulsed with shuddering spasms. The sensual squeeze of her fulfillment triggered his release, taking every last ounce of his energy until he fell into bed beside her, replete.

He didn't know how much time passed before he fell asleep, but he made sure to cover their cooling bodies with the sheets before he smoothed Danielle's tousled hair away from her flushed cheeks. As he watched her sink into slumber, he thanked his personal saints for bringing her to him, all the while wondering why—now that he'd found this incredible woman—she had to be a business competitor. No matter how much she'd claimed to be comfortable with that dynamic, Adam knew their relationship would change when he won the account she coveted.

CHAPTER NINE

DANIELLE TOOK THE longest shower imaginable the next morning, hoping if she let the hot water run over her long enough, eventually she'd figure out a way to resurrect some boundaries with Adam.

But when her fingers had turned to shriveled prunes and she still had no idea what to say when she faced him, she realized she couldn't put off their meeting much longer.

Shutting off the water, she told herself she simply needed to be graceful about the whole thing. Adam had probably been with many women. He would know how to handle the awkwardness of the morning after in a vacation romance in which the people involved weren't looking for a serious relationship. She would simply follow his lead.

Drying her hair with a towel, she admired the Venetian-tile countertops and thick linens. The soaps were the same as in her suite, and she reminded herself to contact the ships purchasing agent since she could provide products that were equally exquisite, with of packaging that complemented the earth tones in the bathrooms.

Somehow thinking about her company helped her pull herself together after a night that left her feeling more than a little vulnerable. She had exposed herself in so many ways—

"Danielle?" Adam's voice called to her through the door.

Her heart jumped, responding to him immediately, even as the rest of her insisted she take her sweet time. Shoving her arms into one of the spa robes on the back of the door, she answered him.

"Oui?"

"Breakfast is here."

Her belly growled an answer she hoped he couldn't hear. She had forgotten what a night of lovemaking could do to a woman's appetite. For that matter, she had forgotten what it did for a woman's skin. Her cheeks glowed with good health today.

Opening the door, she saw Adam dressed in fresh clothes and holding a tray of steaming pots and silver-domed platters. White tulips bent their heads over the rim of an amber glass vase.

"You are an early riser, no?" She followed him to a table in the living area of the suite, memories of last night assailing her as she watched the way he moved across the room, his athlete's body strong and graceful at the same time.

"I thought I would walk around the ship so as not to wake you." He set out their breakfast, pouring two cups of coffee from a silver carafe. "I hope you don't mind, but I picked you up a present with a little American attitude. Just a small thing."

He thrust a gift bag in her direction and she knew a moment's hesitation. Gifts complicated things. But as she burrowed through the tissue paper from the ship's gift shop, she found a pair of pink plastic sandals that made her smile.

"I know you navigated Rome like a pro in heels, but just in case you ever want to travel like an American—"

"*Merci*. My feet thank you and I think they will fit perfectly."

The sandals would remind her of Adam and the informed approach he seemed to prefer in everything but his work.

"I scoped out the label in one of your heels from last night." He held out a chair for her. "Come on over and let me feed you."

She joined him, grateful for his thoughtfulness.

"You have been too kind already. Rome was magnificent yesterday. I'm glad we got to see it together." She would never think of that city without thinking of him.

The scent of fresh rolls and eggs was almost enough to make her swoon. She ate a bit before reaching for her coffee mug.

"I agree. And you don't know how strange it is for a guy like me to take time to sightsee. But honestly, a week ago I was too mired in work to even notice the time, let alone what room I was sitting in or what kind of view was outside the window. I'd forgotten what it was like to take a vacation."

"I hope it is an experience you will repeat." She didn't like the idea of him working that hard.

"Somehow, I don't think my next cruise would be quite the same." He winked at her across the table, but the lighthearted gesture didn't diminish the sincerity she heard in his voice.

It made her heart quicken.

Setting down her fork, she reached across the table to touch Adam's forearm.

"I want you to know I've had a wonderful time with you, no matter where things go from here. I am content to simply have this time together until our cruise ends."

He set down his fork, too, and for a moment she thought he would argue about something she'd said. He took a breath, his forehead furrowed. But then he shook his head and seemed to change his mind.

"Fair enough." He picked up her hand and kissed the backs of her fingers. "But I should tell you that your prediction about the media discovering my whereabouts was all too accurate. Someone with a camera apparently saw us together in Rome."

She froze, not sure what he meant.

He pulled a piece of paper out from under a plate of rolls and handed it to her. It was a page from an Italian tabloid dated this morning and included a picture of them walking arm in arm on a busy street in Rome. Danielle's body was pressed snugly to his side and she gazed up at him with a look on her face that mingled joy with admiration.

She appeared totally smitten with the man who formed the photographic center of the photo, his long stride twice the length of hers as they walked with the city behind them and a swell of pedestrian traffic on either side.

The caption of the photo read, "American mogul lingers with international beauty after an ill-fated courtship with starlet." Next to their photo was a smaller stock shot of Jessica Winslow, along with a story about her arrival in Italy to film a movie.

"She must have a wonderful publicist," Danielle finally managed to say, dismayed at the idea of being watched.

"I wouldn't have even seen the paper except that the woman in the gift shop is Italian and she had a news Web site on her laptop when I went in there to look for shoes."

"Charming." Danielle shoved the paper away, her appetite not quite as robust.

The newspaper article presented serious complications. The fragrance community would be buzzing about this for days.

"You're upset." He released her hand.

"My brother has been overly protective of me since the perfume recipe was stolen. I am thirty-four but he hovers over my life as if I were twenty. If we were simply related and shared Sunday dinners together, I would manage. But we run a business together and that creates a lot of stress for me. I will have five messages on my phone when I return to my suite, and while I would like to write off his concerns as groundless, I have to put Les Rêves first in my life if we are going to recover from the devastation caused by the loss of our last big perfume to a competitor."

"And you think this small side note on a foreign news website will hurt your growth?"

"A man in business who is in the social pages is considered a well-rounded stud. A businesswoman connected to men in the social pages is still considered a scandal at worst or frivolous at best. It is a line I've always walked, because socialites make up my most lucrative customer base. But press like this can disturb that careful balance."

She could tell he understood and recognized the double standard when he did not argue the point.

Standing, Danielle picked up the shoes he'd bought for her.

"I need to return to my room, Adam. I'm sorry."

"Are you sure?" He stood, concern obvious in his sea blue eyes.

"We knew this time together had to be temporary." Her heart hurt to acknowledge the end of their time together, but she couldn't afford to make matters any worse than they already were. She could still control the damage if she walked away from him now. "I just did not realize how short a time it would be."

Retreating into the bathroom to dress, she closed the door behind her, shutting him out.

"WHAT SEEMS TO BE the problem?" Adam asked one of the security officers as he waited with Danielle at a check-in area she'd been directed to by guest services when her room key wouldn't work a half hour later. They had been ushered into a room with about twenty other passengers who were experiencing the same problem.

The crowd was becoming restless. A handful of passengers were angry about having missed a shore excursion because of a problem disembarking.

But Adam figured he had more reason to be agitated than anyone else in the room. Danielle had backed off totally after discovering they'd been photographed together. Apparently, Adam's public moment with Jessica in Corfu had alerted the international press to his presence and created the kind of savory drama the tabloids thrived on—at least for this week. They'd surely be on to something else in a day or two. The timing frustrated Adam. Why did it have to happen after such an amazing night with Danielle?

She stood stiffly in front of him now, waiting for more information on the security issue that had temporarily voided her room key.

"There was a break-in and robbery at one of the Roman museums," the female security guard explained to Adam. "One of the shore excursions from

Alexandra's Dream had just toured the place when it happened, so the Italian police asked us to check if any of our passengers might have seen something."

"Was it the Galleria Borghese?" Danielle had turned around to listen. At the front of the room, another security officer sat at a table asking questions and renewing room keys and identification passes.

"Yes. Were you on the tour through the Villa?"

"No." Adam hoped that would ensure they didn't need to answer a lot of questions. "We tried to visit the park, though, and wondered what was going on over there since our car couldn't make it through the rerouted traffic."

Nodding, the security guard excused herself at a signal from the front of the line. Adam noticed a couple of people ahead of them peel away from the line, perhaps hoping the wait wouldn't be as long later in the day.

"Come on." He took Danielle's arm to propel her forward.

When she said nothing to him, silently moving in response, a surge of irritation coursed through him. Not until this moment did he realize how serious she was about severing the connection they'd only just created.

"You can't simply stop talking to me." He leaned forward to speak softly into her ear.

"I have not stopped speaking to you," she argued, never turning around. "Perhaps I am merely quiet today because I am feeling a little—how do you say?—shell-shocked at the events of the past twenty-four hours."

She peered over her shoulder at him as the line—at long last—began to move.

"I just don't understand—" He jingled his change in his pocket, searching for the right words. "Whatever happened to the idea that there is no such thing as bad publicity?"

He didn't understand how she could let her brother manipulate her like this when she was so smart and articulate about her business. He'd attended a panel discussion she'd given the day they'd been at sea between ports and she had impressed him with the scientific connections she drew between scents and emotions.

"That is a saying made by Americans for Americans. That may be true in New York, but it is not true here. The perfume world is small."

"You mean, elitist and stuffy?" He didn't say it to offend her, but how could she not see the downside of such an insular industry?

"That is not at all what I meant and I am quite sure you know it." Danielle sighed as she edged forward.

Finally, she and Adam were signaled forward by ship security and were cleared after a few questions. Their room keys were reinstated along with their boarding passes, and Adam was glad he'd stood in the line since he hadn't even realized his key card had been affected, as well.

"But you have to admit," Adam pressed, "that to

an outsider, the European fragrance industry might seem a kind of closed society to newcomers. Even Prestige doesn't quite fit in."

That fact was his only misgiving about going after the United Arab Emirates markets. There existed a global bias that sometimes perceived American companies as being too large and impersonal. Occasionally, Adam was subjected to the criticism that companies like Prestige were mercenary for going after new business with capitalistic zeal.

"I cannot speak to that, being an insider. But I can say that some people enjoy working with a small, family-owned company that doesn't have to answer to endless corporate boards and complicated chains of command." She stuffed her key in her bag after getting the all-clear from security. "I don't think there's anything elitist or stuffy about that."

"Danielle, all I'm saying is that you are operating in a very narrow field. Don't get me wrong, it's one that I admire now. But I didn't see its merits until I came on this cruise and experienced it for myself."

He'd bitched and moaned big-time about hanging out with perfume snobs. But the people he'd met were very different from what he'd expected.

Danielle waited, silent. A few other returning passengers moved past them toward the elevators while they remained in the wide corridor.

"You might be glad to break out of your tight business circle some time. Maybe if the company were a little more diversified, you wouldn't feel so bound by the more traditional atmosphere of the fragrance world." He didn't understand why she didn't just tell her brother to go blow, but then he might not have all the facts.

"I understand," she admitted, nodding finally as she readjusted her purse on her shoulder. "But I am not in a position to finance such big moves, much as I might enjoy those opportunities."

Damn. He'd unwittingly injured her pride, forgetting about the financial hardships her company must have suffered after losing an important perfume formula to a competitor.

"Let me at least walk you to your room." He steered her forward through the hallway. "You never told me who this guy was that stole the perfume recipe from you."

He hated the idea of someone deceiving her. Hell, he didn't even like the idea of someone else touching her. Their night together hadn't done anything to ease the desire for her that had been growing ever since his first day on board. If anything, he only wanted her more.

"Does it matter?" She entered the elevator while he held the button.

"Yes, it matters." He followed her inside and pressed the button for the penthouse level. "Don't you think I'd want to avoid doing business with someone lacking in ethics?"

"In that case, his name is Gunther Stahl and his family owns—"

"Panache Fragrances," he finished for her, angry all over again for her sake. "They made a big splash two years ago with the hottest scent of the season. For a virtually unknown company, it was a major success story in the industry."

She looked impressed.

"I see you know more about the perfume world than you let on."

"I know the business." He would have never set foot on the ship if he hadn't been well versed in the financial statements and industry information. "It's the art and science I don't know much about."

The elevator chimed for her deck and he followed her to her suite.

When she swiped her key card, he knew their time together was at an end. Still, he couldn't help but stand on the threshold as she let herself in.

"So why didn't you sue him?" He knew she hadn't. He would have read about it in the industry overview Joe had provided him with before he left the States.

"As you have so eloquently pointed out, Adam, ours is a small business. Those who make trouble find themselves on the outside looking in, a risk we could not afford with Les Rêves. And perhaps my pride would not let me chase down that recipe legally. I told myself if I struck gold once, I could do it again with a new formula that would wipe his off the map." Setting her purse down inside the suite, she faced him. "I will admit it was probably not a wise decision, but it was made in anger."

Her beautiful features were set in determined lines and he regretted that their relationship had dredged up new professional obstacles for her.

"I'm sorry." He skimmed the backs of his fingers along her cheek. "If there is anything I can do to take some of the heat off you this week, just let me know."

She nodded, her eyelids closing for a moment before she backed up a step.

"Thank you. And I'm sorry, too, but I think the best thing for us to do at this point is to simply say goodbye."

CHAPTER TEN

"WHERE THE HELL are you?" Giorgio Tzekas's voice growled through the phone as Mike O'Connor made himself comfortable in a rented vacation villa just up the Italian coast from Civitavecchia that same morning.

Juggling his cell phone against his ear while he looked out at the beach, Mike spotted a woman closing up a boat rental shop. She was carefully lowering a wooden awning over the front window for the midday break.

"I'm in Rome visiting the Pope, didn't you hear?" Mike was damn pleased with the cover that had bought him an extra night off the ship. Security wouldn't be as tight tonight while *Alexandra's Dream* was docked in Livorno.

"Yeah, I heard. Don't you think your story is going to fall through the minute security checks out the people who failed to get on the ship last night? They're looking for leads on stolen goods. Security has been questioning passengers who went into Rome all morning." Giorgio sounded even more tense than usual.

Mike didn't appreciate the third degree when he was the one taking the risks lately.

"I'm on the petitioner's list of people who want to see the Pope." He'd made sure he got on the list to cover his tracks, even though his chances of getting an audience with the Pope were nil. If push came to shove, he'd plead ignorance. Most American priests were far removed from the inner workings of Rome anyhow, so it wasn't as if he would be an automatic suspect. "Besides, security isn't going to be too worried about a priest."

He fingered the small relic in a pocket of his jacket. Last night he'd secured it the old-fashioned way instead of bartering with the kinds of crooks who dealt in antiquities. It had saved him a lot of hassle and it had been a kick to return to his roots. He just hoped the boss didn't find out about his methods.

The clay would not set off the metal detector when he passed through security. As long as no one decided to pat him down, he should succeed in bringing the item aboard. And if anyone found it, he would expound on his joy at being given a gift by the Holy See. It would work.

"Where are you really?" Giorgio pressed. "There is already a crowd of old ladies around the library looking for you. Ariana had to tell them you won't have another lecture until tomorrow. That draws the wrong kind of attention."

Mike was more concerned with the woman

closing up the boat rental spot for the lunch hour, her figure lean and toned even though her dark hair was threaded with streaks of gray. There was something sexy about her out here alone in a quiet fishing village away from the crush of cruise tourists that frequented the bigger coastal cities.

This might be the perfect opportunity to make sure they both found some company.

"Then why don't you help Ariana send the old bats on their way? God knows you've been drooling over that prissy librarian ever since the ship launched. Why don't you buy her tickets to some classical concert or take her to an art museum while you case the place for me? Make a move on her already and stop taking out your lack of sex on me." Impatient to get off the phone before the woman disappeared, Mike opened the door to his villa and headed across the beach with his cell phone in hand.

"Go to hell," Giorgio snarled. "And keep Ariana Bennett out of your dirty-minded thoughts. She's off limits to you."

"Whatever." Mike wondered how he could know ten times more about a woman he didn't even like than the oblivious Giorgio. "I'm calling the boss tonight to say everything's going according to plan. I suggest you make it a point to pass through security tonight around eight o'clock to ensure I get back on board with that…gift…we discussed."

With a grunt, Giorgio finally disconnected the call, leaving Mike to celebrate his small theft with a hot-to-trot Sophia Loren look-alike. She raised her hand to wave and smile at him.

Too bad he realized just then that he was still wearing his collar.

Muttering an oath, he waved back at her and wondered how he could seduce a woman with his priestly cover in place. Definitely a challenge. But would the payoff be even more rewarding?

Years ago he'd worked as an actor. Maybe he'd go for a more brooding approach to see if she was the kind to offer a world-weary priest a once-in-a-lifetime night of forbidden passion to distract him from his heavy burdens. Oh, yeah, he liked the sound of that.

Stifling a smile, he nodded solemnly at her and started calculating how long it would take to get her back to his rented cottage for a few hours.

DANIELLE MADE HER WAY to the library in search of something constructive to do before she lost her mind. After all that had shifted in her life in twenty-four hours, she was worried, anxious about her professional future—and very confused about her feelings for Adam. Feelings she could not afford to think about now. Feelings she had been denying when she told him they needed to stop seeing each other.

Her head pounded with the strain of thinking in circles as she bypassed the English tearoom and continued along deck six, needing to find a colleague, someone to discuss business with to help her forget she was hiding out from the phone and Marcel's calls and his renewed threats to cut off her funding on the Nice store.

He couldn't do that legally. But of course, they ran Les Rêves like a family business, not a faceless corporation, and she'd allowed him free reign with the finances. How could she fight him now? Should she threaten to take him to court? It had always seemed easier to simply work harder to develop the new business he continually pushed her to create.

And so what if that made her a coward? She could not afford to screw up this week any more than she had, and Marcel's renewed frustrations with her— his anger about her public appearance with a well-known American competitor—would only put her off her game when she needed to be sharp.

Focused.

Jonathan Nordham had been in the Rose Petal that afternoon, but Danielle had not joined him because he seemed to be sharing a very intimate cup of tea with the harpist he'd been admiring a few days ago. Apparently, Danielle wasn't the only one to find a shipboard romance, although she might be the only one foolish enough to throw away romance with both hands. Confused and frustrated, she stepped into the library to find the American librarian— Ariana—warding off flirtation from an officer leaning over her desk. Perhaps Danielle wasn't alone in her decision to shun romance after all.

"Excuse me?" she interrupted them, sensing the librarian wouldn't mind an ally.

"Yes." Ariana stood immediately, straightening the items on her desk, which were already in perfect order. "How can I help you?"

"I'll see you at dinner," the officer said to Ariana, backing away with a wink.

Danielle realized by the stripes on his uniform that this was the same man Father Connelly had been walking with a few days ago. The first officer, she thought.

"I am looking for Father Connelly," Danielle began, disappointed she didn't see him in the room. "I had hoped he would share some of his expertise with me."

She wanted to refine her ideas for packaging the Arabian Nights line before she went to Ahmed for their second round of discussions.

"He won't be back on board until tonight," Ariana explained, tucking aside a pair of headphones and a boxed CD set of Wagner's *The Ring Cycle* into her desk. "Apparently he had some appointments with church leaders in Rome and will catch up with the ship just before we sail."

"Is there something I can help you with?"

"Do you have some time?" Danielle appreciated the offer.

"Absolutely," Ariana assured her. "What are you looking for?"

Danielle smiled inside, her heart warming with gratitude for the unexpected help and companionship when she needed it most. Ariana did not know it, but

Danielle feared her heart would break if she allowed herself to think about all she'd walked away from when she said goodbye to Adam.

Focusing on her work now, she withdrew some rough sketches from her purse and began to explain the concept of her perfume line. Ariana nodded and proceeded to reel off a few different ideas based on Arabian myths and legends. Intrigued, Danielle took notes and set off for the communications center to do some research on the Internet.

As long as she concentrated on Les Rêves, she'd be fine. Maybe Adriana's research tips would help her find that magical marketing scheme to captivate Ahmed and International Markets.

She'd work all night on her upcoming presentation. She need to flesh out ideas that she'd only sketched briefly the first time around. She would invest something more, something extra, some small facet of herself into this presentation to ensure she walked away with the account.

Quite simply, she would do whatever it took. Because there was no way a man—however unwittingly—would cost her another prime piece of business. Danielle might have been too trusting the first time around, but she had no excuses now.

Not even the unexpected tenderness she felt for Adam would sway her from her new course.

"YOU'VE NEVER SEEN Livorno? Florence?" The old Englishman, Nordham, posed the question while he and Adam waited for their turn with the simulator on the ship's high-tech practice green.

They stood watching the pair ahead of them compare their shots to the ideal golf swing. Adam had run into Nordham at a workshop on fragrance customization earlier in the day and appreciated the company, but he planned to avoid any mention of Danielle.

How could she have been so quick to cut and run because of a bogus newspaper photo that amounted to nothing in the larger scheme of things? Her brother had to be on the obsessive side to keep such close tabs on his thirty-four-year-old sister. Then again, Adam was an outsider in this industry. Maybe there was some sense to the brother's worries if the fragrance world was as small and traditional as Danielle had suggested.

"No," Adam answered finally while the pair ahead of them cleared the green. "I've never been to either."

"You should go." Nordham stepped up to take his swing next, not bothering to check the monitor. "Florence is Il Duomo. It's *The Agony and the Ecstasy*. Home of Michelangelo. It's…" He paused in lining up his shot to look at Adam. "It's a rare and unique thing."

The older man returned to his putt and sank the shot easily.

Adam couldn't explain that Florence wouldn't be the same without Danielle since he damn well refused to talk about her today, so he settled for a half truth.

"I might lay off the sightseeing for the rest of the cruise. Today is going to be about golf and billiards. Possibly some hoop if I can get a slot reserved on the basketball court."

Nordham frowned while Adam took his place on the green.

"What?" Adam aligned his stance, wondering when he'd last taken an afternoon off to go eighteen holes. "What did I say?"

Nordham laughed. "You Americans. You always want to see how much you can fit in a day. Even your relaxation is scheduled. Yesterday I watched some American passengers disembarking and wondered how they manage to have any fun on their trips when they have an itinerary as long as their arms to follow. Perhaps Danielle can show you the city's high-lights?"

Adam tapped his ball too far to the left at the mention of her name.

Damn.

He leaned on his club like a walking stick, not caring what the video monitor had to say about his crappy shot. The sun beat down on them while Nordham looked at him expectantly. Knowingly.

"Are you not getting along?" Nordham prodded gently while he reached for the printout assessment of Adam's technique. "I don't wish to pry, but she is a lovely girl and you seemed to be enjoying each other's company."

"But she is here on business and so am I, so…"

He shrugged, unwilling to discuss this in any more detail but not wishing to be rude. Nordham had introduced him to several key contacts during the cruise and seemed like a nice guy. "We agreed we needed to spend time focusing on work."

"Yet you both looked very happy at the luncheon yesterday while you were focusing on each other. Life cannot be all work, my friend." He twirled his golf club lightly between his fingers.

"But apparently she's under a bit of pressure from her brother—" Adam stopped himself, not willing to betray any confidences. "If she needs to work, what choice do I have but to respect her decision?"

Adam didn't understand the dynamic between Danielle and her brother or between Danielle and her colleagues, but he understood that she cared what they thought. She cared so much, in fact, she was willing to deny herself—and him—a chance to explore an attraction unlike anything he'd ever known.

Nordham tossed his golf ball up in the air and caught it a few times, the puckered white surface glinting in the hot sun as the golf pro returned from his lunch break, ready to go back to giving lessons to passengers.

Adam stepped off to one side of the open air deck as they left their clubs with an attendant.

"All I know is this," Nordham offered, clapping Adam on the back. "Danielle is a woman full of life, like her mother. She will not thrive if she continues to allow her brother to dictate the way she does business. That is just my opinion, but as an old man I offer the wisdom of many years. You might encourage her to live through her dreams instead of her fears. Maybe then you'll be rewarded by an engagement with a woman instead of the pool table."

Nordham turned in his club at the desk and excused himself to join an elegant older woman dressed in a wide sun hat and long skirt. Adam wondered what Danielle would do if he protested being shut out of her life prematurely. Would he only make her more upset? Or maybe she just needed time to gain some perspective. Never one to back down from the chance to close a deal, Adam started calculating probabilities for the best places to run into her.

DANIELLE DIDN'T KNOW how long she'd been working on sketches for the new perfume bottles. It had grown late, and she was still sitting on the ledge of the Jasmine Spa's aromatic hot tub on the Helios deck. The working conditions weren't exactly ideal since she'd opted to sit on the dark side of the huge sunken pool designed to look like a Roman bath. Mineral water bubbled around her tub, intensifying the scent of the jasmine petals sprinkled in the water. She'd taken this darker sanctuary for just that reason—the scent.

She had brought a candle from her room to compensate for the lack of light. The spa pool was bisected by tall Roman columns, and the side facing the ocean was lit up now, but Danielle preferred the privacy of the interior pool.

Ariana had proven an invaluable source of information with both her personal knowledge of ancient cultures and her familiarity with a key online resource. In no time, Danielle had been surfing through pictures of paintings depicting Arabian history and culture. She had also discovered a new translation of *Tales from a Thousand and One Nights* in the ship's library and read through some of the stories herself. Ariana had even set Danielle up with a feed from an international music Web site so she could listen to traditional Arabic songs.

She had one hour left to sketch before the spa closed for the night. Her pencil lightly shaded the stark rectangular form of a masculine cologne bottle before she filled in the hint of etching she envisioned to look like an astrolabe. She'd already toyed with a recipe for the cologne, which took the low note of Adam's personal scent—hyssop—and blended a few other floral and spice notes native to the Middle East.

She was genuinely excited about her new ideas for the line and couldn't wait to share them with Ahmed at their final meeting. He'd responded well to her suggestions the first time they'd met, encouraging her to expand her concept. By now, she'd invested a great deal of time and thought into the line when she didn't even have a commitment of interest from a retailer or the financial backing of her own company.

Marcel wasn't interested in putting money behind product development even though he expected her to continually produce new business. How had they grown so far apart these last years? The question plagued her while she worked.

And Marcel wasn't her only problem. There was also Adam. She could have been exploring Livorno with him earlier today. Instead, she had purposely stretched out her work to last all day long so she would not waste time second guessing her decision to call it quits.

Obviously her bid to keep her mind off Adam had failed miserably.

She could almost smell the hyssop in the air as she thought of him, the warm masculine scent plying her memories if not her nose. She put down her pencil to indulge herself for just one moment, the sound of the water jets humming in her ears.

"Don't stop now," a voice sounded over her shoulder, rich and deep. "I like watching you draw."

Startled, she closed her notebook even as she realized who had entered the spa. Adam stood behind her, his hair damp as if from a recent shower or swim. He wore khakis and a blue pin-striped shirt without a tie. His sleeves had been rolled up and he looked like he carried a gym bag over one shoulder, although the candlelight made it difficult to see.

"Adam." Her heart tripped at the sight of him and she became aware of her own attire. She had slid into a bathing suit for her trip to the spa, adding a sheer sarong wrap and a fat red rose tucked behind one ear to set the mood for creativity.

Creativity that he might have seen, even though she'd covered her sketchbook.

But then, did she really suspect Adam would be the kind of man to use her ideas against her the way Gunther once had? Adam's company worked in a global marketplace and it hadn't gotten there by stealing competitors' ideas.

She needed to think for herself again and not pass every decision through the filter of Marcel's judgment or her customers' possible reaction. Had it really helped her to be so conservative the past two years?

"I don't mean to interrupt, but—" He stopped, shaking his head. "Hell. Yes, I did. I've been looking for you because I don't understand why we have to ignore each other the rest of the cruise when we were having what I would call a pretty damn good time together up until this morning."

Danielle didn't have the chance to say she could see his point because, he was already launching a new torrent of words.

"Call me crazy, but I thought we had a termination date in mind for this right from the beginning. We're talking ten days together, Danielle, not a year or even a month." He frowned, setting his gym bag on the deck as if to make sure she knew he wasn't leaving. "The fact is, if I can't manage to date one woman consistently for ten days, maybe I'm as much of a jackass player as those social pages would have you believe."

"I can see where that would—"

"And since I can't accept that depiction of myself, I've decided it's time to fight for my rights."

Danielle blinked, surprised at the new turn the conversation—more like a tirade, actually—had taken.

"Your rights?"

"Yes. I'd like to suggest we had a verbal agreement when we set up the ground rules for this relationship. Ten days. No strings." He lowered himself on his knees to eye level with her. "Since this is only the sixth day at sea and I haven't tried attaching any strings to our affair, I would like to suggest you haven't held up your end of the bargain."

"You are taking legal action?" Her mouth lifted at the corner in spite of his hard-headed tactics.

She had to give him points for a novel approach.

"Not yet." He reached to touch the flower in her hair before he skimmed a finger down the side of her cheek. "I'm just giving you fair warning. I want the rest of the days we agreed on—starting tonight."

CHAPTER ELEVEN

ADAM COULD ALMOST HEAR his brother's voice in his head reminding him that romance shouldn't be a competitive sport. Yet here he was, using pushy tactics and making aggressive demands with a woman who deserved better. But damn it, he couldn't pretend to be someone else with Danielle when she'd been deceived by men in her past.

Danielle tilted her head sideways to look at him, the strap of her bathing suit drooping off one shoulder as she put down her sketchbook. Only then did he realize he still touched her, his hand grazing her jaw as he crouched beside her, water steaming up all around them in the spa. He told himself he should back off now that he'd made his case. Unfortunately, listening to advice—even his own—wasn't his strong suit.

"You think you are entitled to the rest of the days we were supposed to have together." She seemed to still be weighing that request. "But you have to realize that life isn't always fair. You could not have achieved so much in life if you believed otherwise."

"Life may not be fair," he agreed, "but I can improve my odds when I hold people accountable for the deals they make. And we agreed on a good time with no strings."

She flipped her hair over one shoulder and pulled her legs out of the water to dry them off on a white spa towel. A woman dressed in a spa uniform hurried toward them to tell them the spa would be closing.

Danielle thanked the woman as she slid into an ankle-length silk bathrobe. "I could hold you accountable then, too, since I would argue that introducing a publicity-hungry ex-girlfriend into the mix counts as a string."

Adam scooped up her sketchbook along with his gym bag, hoping she'd let him walk her to her room. Or his room. Hell, he'd settled for sitting at the bar with her.

"She wasn't a string. More like a small wrinkle."

Danielle cast a skeptical look his way and he thought maybe it would be best to change tactics.

"Okay. Maybe there were some stringlike qualities to that episode," he admitted, holding out his arm for her. "Can I at least walk you back to your room while we renegotiate?"

"I suppose so." She pointed out an elevator nearby and lightly took his arm.

He suppressed the urge to thump his chest with that small victory.

"Did you go ashore today?" He'd missed her.

Missed seeing the sights with her the way they had in Rome.

"No time." She pressed the button for her floor. "I worked all day. You?"

"Not the same without company. I worked on the golf simulator with Nordham for a while, though."

As they arrived on her floor, she withdrew her key from her robe pocket. In the corridor they met a husband and wife Adam recognized from the fragrance conference.

Adam nodded at the couple, but they were both staring hard at Danielle as they passed without comment.

"What was that about?" Adam craned his neck around to watch the two, not caring if they overheard him.

"Remember I told you this is a small industry?" Danielle used her key to open the door. "I'm sure the rumor mill has been busy with gossip that I'm making a spectacle of myself."

She gestured him inside, a fact he was grateful for even though most of his mental energy was being spent trying to figure out the implications of her being photographed with him.

"I don't get it. You're not allowed to date? How is being seen with me so scandalous?" He followed her inside her stateroom and set his gym bag down next to her sketchbook while she disappeared into the bedroom.

"It's not dating that's risqué, it's the fact that I'm

seen as somewhat of a publicity hound myself." She spoke loudly enough for him to hear her in the living area even though she must have been changing clothes in the next room.

He did his best not to think about her naked while he ordered drinks and a few late-night appetizers from room service.

"The truth is out." He finished the order and hit Exit on the TV screen. "You've only been hanging out with me for my eye candy appeal." He wandered out on the balcony to wait for her.

She appeared beside him a few minutes later in a long white dress that tied around her neck, leaving her shoulders bare.

The pang of want that went through him made him catch his breath.

"Eye candy?" She leaned on the balcony rail as she looked out to sea. "The expression doesn't translate so well, I am afraid."

"Forget it." He couldn't take his eyes off her. "It wasn't true anyway."

"Well, I am one of the few fragrance company presidents who actively solicits business through my social crowd, and as much as others may look down their noses at my plebian way of doing business, it has been the most effective sales strategy I have."

"People are jealous of your success." Still, he hated the way that couple had looked at Danielle.

"It's more than that." She turned against the rail to meet his gaze, moonlight spilling over her and making her white dress glow. "My mother died while cliff diving with a boyfriend—a man younger than her. And because she was a painter and a rebel, an outsider in the industry, she had a bit of a reputation. It's one I seem to have inherited because I look like my mother and share some of her more adventurous qualities."

"She sounds like an amazing lady." Adam covered her hand with his. "I'm sorry for your loss."

"Ten years have come and gone, and I still miss her so much." She blinked fast. Nodded. "I try to tell myself to be more like her and not care what the world says. But in truth, I want Les Rêves to succeed even more than she ever did. I can't help but care about my image since it seems to reflect on the company."

Room service arrived just then and Adam answered the door, asking the server to carry a tray outside. They waited for him to open the bottle of champagne Adam had ordered, along with fresh raspberries and a few other fruits and cheeses. And— being true to his roots—a longneck for him. Adam added a few berries to Danielle's glass before the server poured her champagne and left them to their conversation.

"To Les Rêves." Adam lifted his beer bottle to clink against her glass.

"And to ten-day affairs," Danielle added before taking a sip.

Adam stilled.

"Can I take it you're reconsidering the decision to end things early?" The surge of hopefulness surprised him, warning him he cared too much.

"I think at some point I need to reconcile who I am with who I've tried to be for the sake of Les Rêves." She lifted her champagne glass to the moonlight, studying the bubbles surging past the short stack of red berries. "Maybe that time has come."

"Well, hot damn." He lifted his beer again. "I'll drink to that."

Danielle watched his throat contract with each swallow, his strong, masculine body a pleasure for the senses in so many ways. She might be foolish to reverse a decision made less than twenty-four hours ago, but the day had pounded into her the realization that she couldn't go on running her life and her company by committee. She was in charge and she needed to start acting like it.

If Marcel couldn't accept the unique spirit she brought to Les Rêves, she would offer to buy him out over time. He wasn't happy and she was sorry for that. But she couldn't afford to let him water down the way she wanted to run the company. Their mother may have willed them Les Rêves as a shared asset, but all along they'd agreed Danielle would be the president.

She needed to embrace that power before Les Rêves faded into mediocrity that would make neither of them happy.

"Tell me about your family, Adam. You said your

brother is interested in taking over the business. Is your father in poor health? Does your mother have a role in any of the companies?" She would take this relationship deeper in the handful of days they had left together. Forge boldly into their affair and find out what drew her so strongly to this man. If all she took away was a little more self-knowledge and a whole lot of memories, how could she complain?

Any damage done to her professional reputation or her partnership with Marcel had already happened. Spending more time with Adam couldn't make things worse at this point.

"My father is probably in better shape than me, but then he's a big-time overachiever who throws himself into whatever catches his attention, and physical fitness is one of his interests. He travels constantly, buying up businesses, working his employees into the ground and working out in hotel gyms."

"Sounds exhausting." She didn't protest when he poured her another glass of champagne, the vintage a perfect match for her mood. She stole a handful of raspberries from the room service tray and savored their tangy-sweet flavor.

"My dad's a character." Adam stole a few berries from her hand and set her glass on the teak table behind them. "My mother died of breast cancer when I was a teenager, and while Dad was fairly manic before that, he's kept even busier since she died."

"I'm so sorry to hear about your mother." The answering pang in her heart reminded her how deeply it hurt to lose a parent, and Adam had been even younger than her when his mother died. "What was she like?"

Adam reached for the bowl of berries and held it between them. The moon cast a slice of white light across the water, and *Alexandra's Dream* shimmered a misty silver. Activities on the lower decks were breaking up by now, the hard-core partiers heading for the casino or the wine bar.

The quiet of the sea and the night wrapped around them, cloaking their conversation in intimacy. Danielle tried to envision what Adam's mother might have looked like. How proud she would have been to have raised the man standing before Danielle now.

"She was organized. Tough. A great match for my dad. She wouldn't let him get away with dragging us on the road twelve months a year even though that's how he wanted to live. She made sure we went to high school in one city, though other years we'd had tutors to accommodate my dad's travel. Even when she was really sick, she called the shots when it came to my brother and me."

"And she found you a palm-reading nanny." Danielle picked a berry out of the bowl, but Adam took it from her and slipped it between her lips. "She sounds wonderful."

A pleasurable shiver skipped down her spine at the sensation of his finger on her mouth.

"She was. My father started a foundation to

benefit breast cancer research and a handful of other charities after Mom died. A percentage of the company's profits go to the foundation."

"You forgive your father his foibles because he works for a good cause." She understood his family dynamic better now. Possibly she understood him better, too: the loss of his mother might have suppressed his desire to form a long-lasting relationship....

But why did she think about such things when they had firmly committed to their ten days? If Adam ever decided he wanted a long-term relationship, it certainly wouldn't involve her. And yes, she could not deny that fact caused a stab of regret.

"Yes..." He lifted another raspberry to her mouth, the fruit hovering an inch away from her lips.

"But?" She nipped it from his fingers, stealing it away. She would concentrate on what they *could* share together instead of mourning things that would never be.

The rich flavors burst over her tongue, saturating her senses with ripe sweetness. The soft sea breeze pinned her skirt to her legs, teasing her skin with phantom touches even as it carried a hint of Adam's scent. An aftershave, maybe, or a soap.

"The good cause—the foundation—doesn't have to shackle me to one particular job." He seemed to be informing himself as much as her. She didn't know how she understood that, but something in his tone told her he was only just arriving at that conclusion.

"You could donate the proceeds from any endeavor you chose." She wondered if she was losing her touch that he could still be talking about business when her senses were so keenly attuned to him. Dipping into the nearly empty bowl of fruit, she pulled out a small berry and brushed the skin lightly across his lower lip, rolling it beneath her fingers.

"If you ask me," she told him, leaning closer, "you simply need to explore your passions."

He seemed to remember her then, judging by the dark look in his eyes. A flame seemed to light his pupils from within now, the night narrowing to just the two of them on her balcony in the moonlight.

With surprising quickness he pulled the berry into his mouth, swallowing it before he gently clamped her finger between his teeth. The bowl he'd held clattered to rest on a deck lounger as he turned toward her. Into her.

The feel of his teeth sinking softly into her skin tantalized her, making her think about all the ways they could please each other. When a small moan escaped her lips, he released her finger and reached for her hips.

"Guess which passion is first on my list?"

She was too delirious with the feel of his hands on her hips to speak. The heat of his palms penetrated her dress and the decadent silk lingerie she'd slipped on after her trip to the hot tub.

Adam curled his fingers into her flesh with gentle, insistent pressure, pinning her body against his until she felt every square inch of him. His lips grazed her ear, his words soft but distinct.

"If you guess fruit-flavored French women, you'd be right."

CHAPTER TWELVE

ADAM MIGHT PREFER beer to any of the high-brow vintages offered on board the ship, but he had to admit champagne tasted better than anything when tasted on Danielle's lips.

He held her tight against him, shifting her whole body to find the right angle for the kiss. The fabric of her dress was thin and gauzy, allowing him to feel the outline of her underwear just below her waist. His hands were attracted to that line with all the power of a magnet, keeping his touch confined to that narrow pathway.

"Someone will see." Her words drifted through his consciousness as she pulled back to look at him.

His breath heaved in and out of his lungs and he tried to process her words.

"We could move inside," she offered, giving him a clue by nodding toward the door.

"Done." He spun her around in his arms so that she was in front of him and let her lead the way into the suite.

Her dark hair swung against her back as she

moved, the lights from the deck above catching in the dark strands. Everything about her was feminine and graceful.

He didn't let her get all the way to the bedroom, even though he was in a hurry for that. He wanted to take time to appreciate every last inch of her. Now, spinning her in the middle of the suite, he looped his arms around her shoulders, toying with the straps tied at her neck.

"You smell like jasmine," he said.

"I beg your pardon?" Her kick-ass accent seduced him as much as her passion for life. For him.

"Your perfume. I realized tonight when I found you in the spa that jasmine is one of the notes in the scent you wear." Walking into the spa had practically made his knees buckle, the scent reminding him of his night with Danielle. He'd never be able to walk into a florist shop without getting turned on again.

"*Magnifique*. Your skills as a perfumer improve every day." She flicked open a button on his shirt, her fingers cool and light against his skin, which was growing hotter by the second.

"I've been taking workshops. Besides, I'm on a mission to solve the riddle of your perfume." He leaned in closer, brushing his lips over her bare shoulder as he breathed in the scent of her. "But I think I'm going to need some extra time with you to let the notes really sink in."

"You could cheat and look at the bottle on my bathroom counter." She popped another button and splayed her hand on his chest.

"My method is going to be a hell of a lot more fun." He tugged the tie at the back of her neck. "Especially when the places you put perfume are all so tempting."

The halter top slipped down to reveal a strapless lacy white bra...eyelet, maybe? All he knew was that she looked hot. Hints of skin showed through the fabric, teasing him.

"You couldn't possibly know all the places I wear fragrance." She arched back to push the rest of her dress down her hips, but he stopped her, wanting to save that task for himself.

"No?"

"No. I don't even wear a full-fledged perfume. Instead I mix a blend of light essential oils into a lotion that goes...well, everywhere." Her fingers went back to his shirt buttons, and she lingered with the last one above his belt.

"This sounds like more fun than I could have hoped." He backed her against the open balcony door, illuminating her from behind with a white moon glow.

"But you'll never find scent concentrated in any one place." She tugged his shirt from his pants, and the cotton sliding over his abs felt like a prelude to sex.

"Then you have failed your body chemistry test, since the heat of your pulse points ratchets up any fragrance you put there." He bent to her neck to test the theory and inhaled the sweet, sexy scent that was Danielle.

"Clever man. Or perhaps you have just spent more time exploring your lovers' bodies than me."

He licked her neck with a quick swipe of his tongue and her breath caught. Held.

"I promise you'll benefit from the experience." He planted his hands on either side of her, bracketing her with his arms.

"You men are full of promises." She rose up on her toes, forcing his tongue to swipe lower beneath her collarbone. "What I am interested in is the fulfillment of these promises. I believe you call this the 'action' portion?"

Danielle waited for him to see her point, to tumble her into bed and…well, tumble her.

But the man had a will of steel. And, lucky for her, all the rest of him was quite steely, too. She just needed to make him appreciate the urgency of the matter.

Hoping the removal of her clothes would help him see matters her way, she slipped a finger into the waist of her half-fallen dress.

"Danielle." His reaction time was lightning fast. His hands pinned hers to her sides, preventing her from moving. "Wait."

She would rather have been naked, but she definitely didn't mind being pinned by this man. Her skin tingled with pleasure, a warm glow suffusing her whole body.

"Make me." Her challenge tightened his grip, and his pupils dilated ever so slightly in response.

Oh, she liked this.

"I don't want to regret not taking the time to appreciate what's happening between us." His words were harsh. Serious. "I spent all today knowing I'd regret it if I didn't try to see you again in spite of what you wanted. And I kept thinking about how much I wanted to find out where you like to be touched best. I want to know what it will do to you if I touch your thigh under a table full of people or what would happen if I undressed you with my teeth. And I'm going to hate it if I go back to New York next week and still don't know."

Her heart slowed, her pulse slamming with a devastating beat when it finally kicked in. She could get lost in this moment and never resurface. The air between them crackled with sexual energy and keen awareness.

"I—" Her voice was so breathless it barely had a sound. She tried again. "I want things, too. And since there's not a chance I'm testing the theory of what might happen between us if we were in a room full of people right now, I think we'd better explore one of my ideas or else you ought to get those teeth ready to disrobe me."

His grin seemed fierce. Feral. But maybe that was because she only had eyes for the glint of his pearly whites. Her breasts ached as she imagined him peeling off more layers.

"I can give you what you want," he promised. "I just want to make us both aware of what's happening here so that we can recall every last heartbeat in vivid detail when we're back on separate sides of the ocean."

A fleeting vision of herself alone in her Nice shop brought a pang to her heart before she chased it easily away with the presence of here and now. Both of which tantalized her.

"I'm aware," she assured him, breathing him in as she tipped her head back against the door. "I'm very, very present to the moment and the feel of you against me. But I don't want to be present any longer. I want to lose myself totally. Sacrifice my thoughts to an inferno of feeling until there is nothing left but sensation."

He held her there for a moment that seemed eternal, his breath syncing up to hers to create a oneness between them. And then he lifted her off her feet, picking her up right off her shoes to carry her in his arms through the suite to the bedroom. The mental gratification of having made him see her point didn't come close to the physical satisfaction she knew awaited them in this room. The scent of lavender on the sheets drifted up as he tossed her in the middle of her bed. He didn't join her right away and she enjoyed the simmering expectation ignited by watching him unfasten his shirt cuffs.

"I have swayed you from your good intentions." She flexed her leg to wrap around his calf, holding on to him while he undressed.

"I'm a reasonable man." He shucked his shirt and

stretched out over her, putting his weight on his forearms. "Besides that, you make a damn persuasive argument."

His mouth covered hers, silencing any response she might have made. Her words turned to sighs and then a low, needy moan in her throat. She met each swipe of his tongue with a stroke of her own, matching his movements until the warm heat in her womb became something sharper. Something she couldn't ignore.

Her fingers raked helplessly down his sides as she reached for his belt, but he distracted her by slipping a hand behind her back and unfastening the frivolous white cotton eyelet bra she'd bought more for show than function. Her fingers paused at his waist while he lowered the garment, unveiling her breasts.

The night breeze off the water was less noticeable in the bedroom, but she felt it most keenly in the sensitive peaks of her curves as he cupped them each in turn. He drew one taut bud into his mouth and her hips arched in immediate response, the link between pleasure points keen.

Her thighs twitched restlessly until he moved his own leg between hers, providing delicious counter pressure to an ache too sweet to bear.

A wildness took hold of her, making her twist her head back and forth along with her hips. She wanted more. Much more. And she didn't know how long she could wait to find it.

"Please." She clutched his belt with an awkward grip, determination making up for what she lacked in finesse. "I am…" The words evaporated from her mind. "Urgent."

He must have listened because he began to work his way down her body, lowering the skirt of her dress with his teeth. The feel of his breath so close to her skin made her edgy. Excited. Frantic.

When he pulled the fabric over her hip she nearly came undone and he hadn't even touched her. The dress wound around her knees, binding her in place while he slid back up her legs to retrieve her panties.

Merde.

She battled the urge to close her eyes and let sensation carry her away because she did not want to miss anything. Her fingers twined in the sheets as he hovered over her, teeth clamping on the elastic at her waist. Fire raged over her skin, the heat concentrated at the juncture of her thighs. When he unwound her dress from her legs and planted an intimate kiss there, she cried out with the pleasure of it. The sweet sensation rained over her, quenching the fire on her skin and bathing her nerve endings in undiluted bliss. She quaked with the force of her release, her whole body shaking from lush spasms.

Caught up in her own fulfillment, she must have missed Adam taking off the rest of his clothes and making sure they were protected. She regretted her sexual selfishness as he stretched out over her, naked and ready, while she floated on a cloud of ecstatic aftershocks.

But heaven help her, she couldn't regret it for long as he slid inside her. Filling her completely. She wound her arms around him, her legs around him. He steadied her, adjusted her, and then found a way to slide still more deeply within her.

Tunneling her fingers through his hair, she kissed him. That simple, elemental joining was all she could contribute to their coming together since the rest of her body was completely in thrall to whatever he wanted and however he moved. Her fingernails scraped his shoulders as he withdrew from her and then pushed his way back again. Deeper. Sweeter.

The rhythm took her again, hot and fast. Finally she understood why Adam wanted to slow things down. She wasn't ready for this to end, either. She tried to hold back, desperate to keep him deep inside her, desperate to put off her release, which was so close. So inevitable.

So—

The tide crashed over her, battering her with wave after wave of molten heat. The ship beneath her could have been sinking and she wouldn't have known it, her whole world narrowed to the feel of Adam in and all around her. His completion followed hers by seconds, minutes maybe, but it seemed those heightened sensations went on and on. The thrill of each new sensual shudder traveled back and forth between them, multiplying.

She might have fallen asleep in that haze of sexual contentment if Adam hadn't moved her, securing a pillow under her head and covering her with the sheet. She curled into him then, grateful she had not shut him out of her life this week.

"I will not regret this," she murmured through sleepy contentment, determined she would find a way to pull her company together, with or without a public image the world approved.

"You'd better not." He slid his arm underneath her pillow while his other hand fell into the crook of her waist. "Or I'll hunt you down in France and remind you exactly why this was a good idea."

She smiled for a moment before a pang shot through her heart. Not seeing him again after this cruise would be a higher price than she'd originally foreseen.

The thought troubled her as she recognized yet another problem in her life she didn't know how to solve.

CHAPTER THIRTEEN

"How do you feel about darts?"

Adam posed the question from Danielle's bed two mornings later while he watched her hurry around the bedroom searching for a misplaced lipstick, a mate to a shoe and a hairbrush in quick succession. He liked seeing this side of her—the private side that was more whirlwind than sophisticated European. They had barely left her suite in thirty-six hours other than a quick jaunt into Portofino. Although the Italian Riviera had appeal, it couldn't compete with dragging Danielle back to bed.

She paused long enough to peer strangely at him.

"Darts?" Her accent softened the *d* almost to a *j*, the game clearly unfamiliar to her.

"Yeah. A game where you throw, uh—they're like miniature arrows—at a corkboard to score points. A bar game."

Finding the missing shoe under her bed, she slipped into her high heels. She wore an olive-colored linen skirt and a gold camisole that showed off an abundance of skin. He wanted to haul her back into bed but she had her second formal meeting with Ahmed Ramnathan this morning and he didn't want to do anything she might perceive as jeopardizing her chances of landing the account. He planned to give the retailer his best shot, too, and he wanted a clear conscience about how the business deals shook down when the cruise was over.

"I'm afraid I have missed the kinds of bars where arrows are slung about." She reached for her jacket and Adam mourned the loss of a spectacular cleavage display. "But I am a woman of adventure, so perhaps you can show me later when we go ashore."

Villefranche was the port closest to Danielle's home city of Nice and the site of her satellite shop. He had to admit he was curious to see her on her home turf later today.

"You'd try darts for me?" He tried to picture her in her heels and designer clothes lining up in front of the dartboard.

She shrugged as she swiped on a peachy-colored lipstick and assessed herself in the mirror.

"You sniffed flowers and ferns with me. Why would I not give miniature arrows a try for you?"

He had to grin at that.

"That might be the most romantic thing a woman has ever said to me." He shoved off the covers and rose out of bed since she appeared close to leaving. He'd already showered—an event he'd never forget since he'd taken Danielle in with him—but he hadn't bothered to dress yet since he didn't want to miss a moment of watching her.

"Stick around." She turned smoky eyes his way and looked at him through long lashes, her painted lips puckering in a full-on pout. "Romance is what a French woman does best."

He skimmed his hands over her hips and up under her jacket to the delicate silk of her camisole and the soft skin beneath it. In deference to her newly painted lips, he planted a kiss beneath her ear, tasting his way down her neck.

Her fingers clutched at his shoulders and he had to stop himself from pulling her back into bed and messing her up all over again.

"Good luck with your pitch, Danielle." He stared down into her eyes, until she blinked away the heated moment and stepped back.

"Thank you." She smoothed her skirt and picked up her sketchbook.

"You must know I accidentally saw a few of your drawings the other night at the spa and they look fantastic. Ahmed would be an idiot to ignore that kind of tailor-made marketing effort for their UAE customers." In the name of fair play, Adam thought he should at least admit that he'd gotten a peek at her work.

A frown pulled at her lips for a moment before she seemed to shake it off.

"I'm really excited about the potential for the

line," she admitted, sliding the spiral book into a leather bag with some other paperwork. "I based the ideas on *Tales from the Thousand and One Nights*."

"It's a great idea." He noticed she didn't offer him a second glimpse, obviously uncomfortable with sharing any more details than necessary.

It sucked being competitors like this.

"You must be pitching something equally unique."

He recognized a subtle hint for more information and didn't see the harm in telling her his plans, especially since he'd inadvertently glimpsed some of hers. Maybe the shared information would put her more at ease.

"Prestige Scents is actually taking the direct opposite approach. Instead of catering to the roots of Arabic culture, we're bringing in some of the tricks of the West and pitching a celebrity as the face of perfumes we'd sell there."

Danielle bit her lip, clearly uncomfortable talking business.

"Perhaps Jessica? Hmm. Not that I begrudge the little box-office darling an ounce of her success or anything."

She said it with such a complete lack of sincerity, he couldn't help but laugh.

"No. We won't firm up a face or an image until we progress in negotiations, and we haven't ruled out a regional celebrity." Adam was still working the deal. And he felt a twinge of guilt since he could see for himself that Danielle's campaign had taken far more work. But no matter how inspired her scheme was, he still felt really good about the financial projections of his own plan.

"Thank you for telling me." She picked up her room key and added that to her bag, her movements clipped. Tense? "It's been hard for me not to talk about my ideas for the Arabian Nights line since my work permeates my whole life. When I am creating something new, I tend to think about it waking and sleeping."

He saw a ticket out of this conversation and ended it, ready to move their relationship back on comfortable—hot—terrain.

"I'll bet I know a few times when you weren't thinking about it."

He'd never been with a woman who committed herself so completely in the bedroom. He didn't tend to romanticize relationships, but being with Danielle gave new meaning to the idea of being transported during sex.

"I do, too, you wicked man, and now I'm feeling a bit frazzled walking into a meeting when I haven't been going over my notes or—"

"Don't." He cut her off with a finger gently pressed to her lips. "You've got more time and creativity invested in this pitch than I do and—I'm willing to bet—anyone else Ahmed is seeing this week. Your ideas are kick-ass. Go sell the hell out of them."

And he meant it. He could take a little competition. Hell, to hear his brother talk, Adam thrived on it. No way would he want Danielle to do anything less than her best.

Her whole body seemed to relax at his words. When she nodded and smiled, he felt like a freaking hero.

"I will. Thank you." Pivoting on her heel, she walked away from him, pausing at the threshold of the door to her suite. "You're going to love Villefranche and we can tour the city well into the evening since we have a late sailing. Why don't you ask someone in guest relations to recommend an establishment with darts?"

"I'm on it." He didn't bother telling her that anything guest relations would recommend in Portofino would undoubtedly be more upscale than the dive bars he frequented in his free time.

Besides, he was already thinking about her nonstop when he had work to consider, and that wasn't such a great thing. He knew his proposal could win this deal, but not if he was so rocked by a woman that he didn't have all the details smoothed out by the time he went into that final meeting tomorrow. Danielle's proposal was excellent, but she was a savvy enough businesswoman to know that Prestige had a lot more tools besides artistic creativity to bring to this deal.

Adam's phone showed two messages from Joe. No doubt his brother had projects Adam needed to start thinking about for next week when he rejoined the rat race.

Yet if Adam discovered that Danielle was not only a sexy businesswoman who could match wits with him any day, but a born dart player…he might never get on the plane to fly home.

DANIELLE MADE A DETOUR to the ship's library before her meeting with Ahmed to return her copy of *Tales From a Thousand and One Nights*. She'd left her room early to drop off the book, but it had not been easy with Adam almost naked and lounging around her bedroom.

Mon Dieu.

The man was too delicious for words. No wonder women pursued him around the globe. If she wasn't careful, she'd be the next woman to fall hopelessly under the spell of his easy charm and his American accent.

The sound of raised voices from the library startled her as she neared the room. Ariana had said the reading area would be closed to passengers this morning, but that she would be there, so it unsettled Danielle to hear the raised masculine voice booming through the closed door.

"—know how hard it is to find good quality copies? Even high quality reproduction pieces are—"

Danielle rapped on the door, spying Ariana in the far corner of the library through a clear sidelight in the door.

The male voice fell silent as Ariana hurried over to let Danielle inside. Danielle nodded her thanks and a greeting, but she didn't turn in the book right away, wanting to make sure Ariana didn't need help dealing with an angry patron or—

Father Connelly?

The normally affable priest was standing by his antiquities display, a piece of painted pottery shattered at his feet in a rainbow of colors.

"Is everyone okay?" Danielle asked, hoping no one had been cut. "What happened?"

Ariana pushed her dark hair behind her ear, a steaming cup of coffee in one hand.

"Someone on the cleaning staff broke one of Father Connelly's display pieces," Ariana confided, keeping her voice low. A maid arrived just behind Danielle, but Father Connelly waved the woman away while he paced along the far wall outside the circle of scattered pottery.

"It was the Olympian vase, no?" Danielle thought she recognized the piece from the lecture she'd attended.

"Yes," Father Connelly replied tightly, not bothering to look her way. His Roman collar was askew, his hair sticking up in the back.

"I have a few friends in the art business," Danielle offered, hoping to defuse the tension. "I can ask one of them for the name of someone who does skilled reproductions in this time period."

That caught the priest's attention. As he approached her, she noticed Ariana step back and quickly pick up a fragment of the vase. Did she hope to hide her action from the priest? Instinctively, Danielle trusted the librarian, who had been more than kind to her in her research efforts. Danielle had succeeded in drawing out the quieter woman after the library had closed to the public. She hadn't realized until then how much she missed having a friendship that didn't revolve around her work.

"That's very kind of you." His smile was tight. "But it won't be necessary. I will contact a few of my suppliers and find something appropriate to supplement the collection. I just regret the expense for a replacement. I'd much rather add something new to the collection instead."

Smoothing a hand over his hair, he seemed to recover himself.

"I just wanted to return this book to you." Turning to Ariana, who had come back to stand with them, Danielle passed her the book. "Now, if you both will excuse me, I have a meeting I must attend."

"Of course." Father Connelly smiled. "*Adieu, mademoiselle.*"

"*Adieu.* And thank you, Ariana. Your help has been invaluable to my project this week."

"It was my pleasure, Danielle. I appreciated your company."

Danielle left the mess in the library to meet with Ahmed. Her hopes were high even though she knew Adam's pitch probably had as much chance of winning the contract as hers. And damn it, that worried her. She couldn't afford to lose this deal. Her shop in Nice depended on it. Her whole company might depend on it if Les Rêves's financial prospects were as bleak as her brother had been painting them lately.

But at this point, she could only work with what she had. Still, she was nervous. Her company would be devastated if she lost the bid to Adam. But after spending another incredible night with him, she recognized she would be the one who suffered if she lost her heart to him.

ADAM'S CELL PHONE RANG in the middle of the afternoon. Since they'd docked in Villefranche, he'd already fielded two calls from his brother, who had arrived in Europe yesterday on business of his own.

Now, Adam ducked into a window seat in the main lounge area where a piano player worked the keys of a baby grand. The lounge was relatively empty since most passengers had gone ashore for the day and many of the perfumers were attending afternoon workshops. Adam had enjoyed the speaker on neuroesthetics who looked at the scientific particulars of the brain's response to scent.

"Burns." He didn't recognize the number on the call window.

"Why aren't you still in my bed?" The sexy voice on the other end of the phone could only belong to one woman.

His mouth watered within two seconds of thinking about Danielle. Too bad the workshop on neuroesthetics hadn't included some explanation for the way his brain responded to Danielle. Now that would have been intriguing.

"I didn't know when you'd be back." He had left her room moments after she did that morning, hoping to tweak his own presentation before returning his brother's calls. "But if you're not busy now, I can be there in five minutes."

He only had three days with her left, counting today. And really, today was half over. He planned to make the most of every moment remaining on this cruise.

"Have I told you how much I love your American impatience?"

"You might be the only one." He stared out across the water at the coastline. "What's your take on American football?"

"I have a friend who always manages to secure World Cup tickets. You want to go next year?"

So much for their compatibility.

"That's not American football."

"Football is football, no?"

"No. Your football is soccer. Mine involves helmets. Hitting." He waved away a waitress who paused at his table. "How did your meeting go this morning?"

He'd meant to ask that as soon as he spoke to her again, but her sexy voice had distracted him.

"It went better than I could have hoped." She sounded pleased. Relaxed. Happy.

"I'm glad for you." And he meant it. "But what about getting together? Do you want company?"

His second appointment with Ahmed was tomorrow so he had today free if he ignored Joe's dictates.

"How about we just go ashore early? I'll dress now and—"

"Dressing is optional if I come over there." He nodded at Jonathan Nordham, the Brit with the brandy flask who'd given him excellent advice about trying to work things out with Danielle. The semi-retired perfumer was with his lady friend.

"Maybe we should meet on deck then so you don't miss Villefranche altogether. How about an hour from now in the Polaris Lounge?"

The connection clicked and he guessed she must have another call coming in so he wrapped things up.

"Done. See you then." He pressed the button to finish the conversation before he picked up an incoming call of his own.

"Breaking hearts on two continents now, I see," Joe barked into his ear without preamble. "Why didn't you tell me you were making the European papers with your love life?"

Adam spat out a few choice words in reply, knowing Joe must have seen the photo of him with Danielle somewhere. Changing the subject, he watched the first mate and the antiquities lecturer exchange a few terse words before walking away from each other.

"I thought you were too incapacitated to fly,"

Adam accused. "What happened to all the broken ribs?" He couldn't be too mad at Joe—if Adam hadn't taken the cruise he would never have met Danielle.

"I was too incapacitated to take a ten-day cruise and meet with a potential client I'd never dealt with before," Joe clarified. "But I can hold meetings with some of our overseas management—people I don't have to impress. Plus, it's been a few days. I'm getting around better. Thanks for asking."

"I've got my second meeting tomorrow with the retail company. The presentation is solid."

"And judging by the picture I saw of you and the perfume heiress, I'd say you're scouting the competition fairly well."

"Did you want anything business-related, or are you calling to gossip like a schoolgirl?"

"I just found it surprising you'd be making the rounds with the pampered heiress type after Jessica caused you so much grief."

His temple ticked as tension threaded through him.

"Danielle's not like that."

She didn't just shoot around the globe on a moment's whim or change boyfriends as frequently as she changed hairstyles. Adam knew better than to get involved with a woman like that.

"I don't know, bro. Her dating bio in the paper reads like a who's who of European big shots. Then there's a polo player and some kind of D.J.—"

"Enough." His jaw tightened as he remembered

her easy acceptance of his explanation about the kiss from Jessica in Corfu. Didn't he owe Danielle as much benefit of the doubt? "Since when do we trust any b.s. that shows up in a newspaper? She's as much a target as me."

Although it would have been nice if Danielle had spelled that out for him a little more thoroughly. He hadn't realized she'd been linked to a string of high-profile men.

"Whatever. I'll meet you in Piraeus when the ship comes in and we can fly back together. Don't forget what you're there for." The call disconnected before Adam could tell his brother off.

Damn. He switched off his phone for the night, determined to enjoy his time with Danielle. They were sticking to their agreement. A shipboard fling. No strings. No expectations.

Too bad it was all going to blow up in their faces when one of them lost the Dubai deal. Adam knew it. She knew it. But there wasn't a chance he could back away from her or from the inevitable explosion before then.

"HELLO?"

Danielle took the call on her other line, her head still swamped with visions of what she'd do with Adam when she got him all to herself tonight. She needed to wear something spectacular. Something he'd never forget.

Something to soothe her small feelings of guilt

since she was almost certain she was going to win the contract they both wanted now that she'd had her meeting with Ahmed. The Dubai rep had loved the Arabian Nights ideas and thought it would be a big hit with International Markets.

She hoped Adam would not be too disappointed.

"Danielle." Marcel's voice burst her happy bubble, his serious tone calling her back to reality. "We need to talk. Are you alone?"

The tension in his voice put her on guard. He did not just sound a little testy, as per usual. He sounded downright somber.

"Is everything okay?" Her mind raced through a litany of possibilities and she wondered if something had happened to one of the long-time staffers, who were like family to her and Marcel by now.

"No." The word was so sharp she sank to the love seat in the sitting area of her suite, bracing herself for whatever might be wrong. If it had been just a magazine article about her escapades or another turn of the rumor mill, he would raise his voice and chew her out. This quiet tension meant something else.

"You're scaring me." Suddenly her good news about her encouraging meeting with Ahmed and International Markets didn't seem that important.

"I'm vacating my post with Les Rêves, Dani." His voice hitched oddly. "I cannot be the company's financial officer anymore."

She relaxed marginally, grateful the news hadn't been worse. As much as she appreciated Marcel's contributions to the company, she would never want him to remain in a position he found unfulfilling.

"I know you have been worried about money, but *mon Dieu*, Marcel. I thought you were terribly ill or—I don't know. Please do not scare me so—"

"There's more."

She tensed once more, the Mediterranean sunshine outside her French doors feeling a million miles away.

"Oui?"

"I wanted to warn you about our financial situation before the cruise ends in case there is still time to fix the problem."

Her scalp tingled with foreboding and she had the feeling her date with Adam was going to have to wait.

"What problem?"

"I have made so many mistakes, Dani." His words came out in a gasp like a man fighting for breath.

"What mistakes, Marcel?" Anxiety was making her hoarse.

"Our finances are strained. It is my fault. I have been struggling with guilt but I needed to tell you before you make any commitments that the company cannot fulfill."

Her stomach tightened into a solid knot of raw tension.

"Our finances are *strained?*" What did he mean? And how was that different from the financial woes he always griped about?

How could Les Rêves possibly be in a position where they wouldn't be able to fulfill the contracts she secured?

"Our accounts have dwindled. I made a couple of bad investments a few years ago and somehow those losses led to more until I needed a little help from the business." His voice broke now. "We're operating in the red now, Dani. I can't fix this and I can't hide it anymore."

Shock steamrolled her and her legs wobbled with the weight of it. Her brother had invested company money without consulting her? To the point of… what? Bankruptcy? A million thoughts bombarded her brain as she tried to process what he was telling her.

Yet she couldn't do anything until she got a better feel for what was happening. She needed to take action. Now. She didn't need Marcel to give her the details—she knew that her beloved company was at risk.

She wouldn't be able to see Adam tonight. For that matter, she'd be lucky to even say goodbye to the man she'd been so eager to be with just a few moments ago.

How could one phone call change your life so irrevocably?

"I'm coming to Paris, Marcel." She checked her watch, surprised to notice her hand shook ever so slightly. "I can be at your house in a few hours if the flight schedules are favorable. I want to see you and I want to see the books."

Thankfully, she had some reserved funds of her own to use for a flight. Although, maybe she should start being more frugal if the business needed an influx of her personal cash. Dear God, there were too many things to think about.

Not waiting for her brother's answer, Danielle disconnected the call and phoned the airline to change her return ticket.

Because if there was any way to save Les Rêves, even if it cost her every penny of her own cash, she would do it in a minute. And if not, well, if her business was going down in flames, she wanted to at least be there when it happened.

CHAPTER FOURTEEN

ADAM HAD BEEN WAITING fifteen minutes for Danielle when he figured he'd better go back to his room and grab his cell phone. He'd wanted to leave the phone on the ship so they wouldn't be interrupted. It hadn't occurred to him she might stand him up.

Now, clicking through his messages in his suite, he came to one from her that she'd left him almost half an hour ago.

"Adam." A-*dam*. There was a lot of background noise in the call, making her soft accent difficult to hear. "I am catching a plane to Paris. Marcel called and—I have to go. I will catch up with the boat in Marseilles, maybe. I am not sure. I am sorry and— I'm sorry."

The staticky call disconnected abruptly, leaving him to wonder what in the hell had happened. She'd just taken off for Paris without seeing him in person to say goodbye? It had to be something serious. He had his meeting tomorrow with Ahmed—the deal-making meeting that had been his main goal for the trip—so he couldn't chase after a sexy Frenchwoman to Paris.

But what if it meant he'd never see her again? She hadn't sounded all that certain she'd finish the cruise. The thought blindsided him.

He'd given other women the slip without thinking twice about it. But having Danielle up and disappear on him was another matter altogether. His brother's words about Danielle being as much of a pampered heiress as Jessica came back to taunt him now.

Damn it.

If Joe was here, he'd probably also tell Adam to quit being so competitive. He didn't have to chase Danielle to Paris just to prove he could. Just to show her he wasn't as dispensable as the other guys she dated.

But then, Adam wasn't Joe. And Adam didn't have to make the same choices as his brother.

With that justification he was comfortable picking up the phone to tell the family's pilot to meet him in Portofino. The jet was still in Europe waiting for Joe to finish his business there. Adam's competitive streak was an infinitely more convenient excuse for what he was about to do than what he feared might be the real reason.

He was falling ass-backward for a socialite perfumer who seemed to be beating him at all the games he knew best.

But then maybe he was addicted to competition. One thing was certain: Adam didn't plan to let Danielle get away without acknowledging the winner in this game—both professional and personal.

IN HER FANCIFUL imaginings, Danielle floated like a ghost through the house where she'd grown up. She was here, in the Chevalier family's Paris home, walking the maze of halls she had ridden her scooter through as a child. Yet somehow she felt detached from it all, surreal, as if suddenly realizing what a fragile grip she had on security was forcing her to disassociate with all the things she might lose as a result. And while Marcel lived in the home that had been willed to them jointly, Danielle had always known it was here, waiting for her to return to its overrun gardens and views of the Seine on holidays and the occasional weekend.

Sliding back into her seat at the massive country kitchen table, she gripped her newly warmed cup of coffee and stared at the numbers in Marcel's ledgers, trying in vain to find a way out of the nightmare. She didn't need a degree in accounting to see the way the company's assets had been slowly depleted even before Gunther had stolen her perfume recipe. Marcel's bad investments had already started to leak Les Rêves of its profits by then.

"Dani?" His voice called to her from a few rooms away but she didn't answer. Couldn't muster the necessary calm spirit to talk to him when she battled so much anger at his deception.

He'd manipulated her feelings of guilt so skillfully these past couple of years, harping on her poor judgment in trusting Gunther as if that had put the biggest financial burden on them. Danielle could see for herself now that the trouble went deeper. Gunther's white-collar theft had shaken Marcel because her brother knew it would reveal his deception all the sooner.

"I'm in the kitchen," she called back, not wishing to fight over something that couldn't be undone.

But then, she wouldn't hide from it, either.

"There's someone here to see you."

Surprised, she rose from her seat, curious to see who would be here. No one knew she was in town. Except for—

"Gunther?"

Her jaw fell open at the sight of the man suddenly standing in her brother's kitchen, her brain unable to comprehend his presence in this house after all the other nasty surprises she'd received today.

"It's nice to see you, Danielle." Her former lover looked every inch the international playboy in a dark suit jacket over a black silk shirt. His boots possessed a sheen so bright she could probably check her makeup in them. But what struck her as most ostentatious and silly were the fingerless driving gloves encasing his tanned, smooth hands.

Mon Dieu, but she missed Adam and his straightforward approach to everything in life. He'd called himself a WYSIWYG guy—what you see is what you get.

Too bad no one else in Danielle's life seemed to abide by that credo.

"Please tell me you did not dress like such a pretty

boy when we dated." She sat back in her chair, seeing no need to give this man a greeting. "Marcel, you may see him out."

She did not know why her brother had let him in to begin with.

"Dani." Her brother spoke quietly. "He may be able to help."

She whipped her head up to glance at her brother. He stood pale and thin next to Gunther's too-slick good looks.

"What?" She slapped the ledger closed. "My ears must be deceiving me since you have made it a point to paint this man to be the devil himself in every conversation we have had the last two years."

She ignored Gunther's attempt to protest, his presence a non-factor as far as she was concerned. He did not warrant a second glance, let alone any more of her time, when her life was threatening to fall apart.

"Gunther's family has approached us about possibly buying out the company," Marcel explained. His dark eyes, inherited from their father, were somber.

Anger ripped loose the restraint on her tongue and she could not remember ever feeling so much animosity for her brother. Where was his sense of honor? His family loyalty?

Perhaps being with Adam this week had reminded her that honorable men existed. She did not have to be grateful for Marcel's grudging help with Les

Rêves when he'd never embraced the business. She could work with someone else who would respect her and respect the company's goals.

"He approached *us*, Marcel? Or did he perhaps approach *you*, the only one who had an inkling that the company was falling to pieces and might need financial help?" Her heart ached that her own brother could do this to her. "How dare you bring this traitor into the house the very day you unveil three years' worth of mismanagement and deception on your part?"

Gunther whistled softly between his teeth. "You always were the fiery one, Danielle."

Fighting the urge to slug him, Danielle kept her focus on her brother, whose betrayal hurt far worse than Gunther's ever had.

"I will not sell the company. Not today. Not tomorrow. Not ever." She spoke slowly so that both men could understand. With shaking hands, she went to the coffeepot and carried it to the table to refill her cup.

In the ensuing moment of silence she heard a distant pounding on the front door.

"And who might this be? The tax collector? Someone to drag us off to debtors' prison?" She brushed past her brother and tore through the house, determination firing her steps along with a well-deserved bit of fury. "Well, you can all go because I am not admitting defeat."

Crossing the marble tiles of the blue-and-white

foyer her mother had designed with so much care, Danielle prepared to tear into whoever else Marcel had invited to this premature funeral for the business she loved.

She flung open the door, rebuff dying on her lips as the latest visitor came into sight.

"It cannot be."

Danielle stepped back from the man who had made love to her the night before. The man who had insistently pursued her despite her fears that he could betray her the same way Gunther had.

"I assure you it can be." He wore cargo shorts and a T-shirt that smelled like the ship's laundry detergent. His smile tweaked her insides, melting a fraction of her anger for an instant before she spotted his convertible Mercedes coupe in the driveway and remembered why he must be here, too.

Money. Hadn't Marcel told her specifically to make contact with the Prestige Scents representative on board *Alexandra's Dream?* Adam was a potential buyer.

"You have come a long way for nothing." Her heart ached with fresh hurt that did not have anything to do with business and everything to do with her feelings for Adam. "No matter what my brother might have told you, Les Rêves is not for sale."

"Who is this?" Marcel's voice drifted over her shoulder and she turned to find that he and Gunther had followed her into the foyer.

"Wait a minute." Adam shook his head and

stepped inside the house, uninvited. "What are you talking about?"

He directed the question to Danielle, ignoring Marcel.

"I've already negotiated a fair price." Gunther had spoken French earlier, but now he switched to English. He moved closer to stand next to Danielle, practically barring the way into the house with his body. "You can't just come waltzing in here now with some bogus offer to drive up my price."

Danielle spun on her heel to face him. His cologne grated her senses and she wondered if she'd ever be able to use musk in a man's fragrance again.

If she was fortunate enough to stay in the business, damn it.

"You have no right to be in this house, Gunther."

"Marcel invited me to discuss business—"

"Unfortunately, Marcel no longer has a say in the business or in this house since he has frittered away all of his inheritance." She wondered if there was fire shooting out of her ears yet. If there wasn't now, she felt certain it would begin soon. "Get out and do not darken the doorstep ever again or I will call the police. *Comprenez-vous?*"

The expression on his face contained a frightening amount of rage, making her glad for a moment that Adam was here. Even if he wanted to buy her business out from under her, she still felt certain he would never allow some jet-set Euro-trash perfumer to slug her in her own home. There was a core sense of honor in him that Gunther lacked.

"You heard her." Adam's voice was low and threatening, his words a complement to Danielle's sending Gunther out of the house and into the night.

"Danielle—" Adam began.

"I cannot." She had all she could do to hold herself together emotionally right now. Her brother's betrayal, her whole future called into question, Adam's arrival for reasons she hadn't yet discerned...it was all too much. "Please. You will both excuse me. I do not wish to talk."

Taking what few scraps of her pride she had left, she headed for the stairs to seek out her old bedroom and figure out what to do now that her whole life had imploded.

"ARE YOU GOING to run now, too?"

Marcel Chevalier's question stopped Adam as he walked down the front steps to leave the house, Paris and Danielle behind.

He might be falling for her, but if she didn't want to talk to him, he wasn't going to make things tougher for her. She was obviously facing some kind of business crisis he didn't know anything about.

And didn't it suck to realize how little of her life she'd shared with him? Maybe they had been living a freaking fairy tale on board the ship and the shine would wear off their feelings once they were back in the real world. Hell, it already seemed to be happening for her.

Turning on his heel, he faced Danielle's brother, a slight man with dark eyes and light brown hair, his only resemblance to his sister in the shape of his face.

"What the hell is that supposed to mean?" Adam glanced down at his feet. "Doesn't look to me like I'm *running* anywhere."

"You're leaving. It's the same thing." Marcel folded his arms defensively across his chest and propped a shoulder against a polished grandfather clock a good foot taller than him.

"Not quite." Adam didn't want to argue with this guy. Now that he looked closer, Danielle's brother seemed ready to fall apart. "Is what Danielle said true? Did you piss away your part of the inheritance?"

He stood outside in the last rays of sunlight on a long summer day. It had to be nine o'clock by now and the outdoor lights had flipped on a few minutes ago even though it wasn't fully dark yet. The houses in this part of town—technically the outskirts of the city, according to Adam's pilot—were not mammoth mansions, but everything about them said old money, from the Greek revival stone architecture to the landscaping and the cast-iron light fixtures hanging over the terrace area.

"*Oui*. Danielle only just found out about the money." Marcel pushed away from the clock and peered behind him at the staircase where Danielle had disappeared, then he followed Adam outside onto the terrace. "Maybe I should sell this house and invest the profits in the company. I don't know. But I couldn't make any more decisions without consulting her."

Adam wondered what exactly had happened, but wasn't sure how much he should push. Danielle had seemed pissed that her brother had confided in Gunther.

How unreal was that? Her old boyfriend had been here with her when Adam showed up, a circumstance that might have given him pause with other women, but he hadn't felt a second's worth of jealousy because he trusted her. Understood her better after a handful of days together than he'd understood other women after year-long relationships.

"I don't get it. You ripped off your own business?" So much for not pushing. Adam wanted to be able to put the pieces together. If Danielle was checking out on him this week anyhow, he wanted to at least know what had happened.

"I made a few bad investments with company money in an effort to offset some of our setbacks."

"Bad investments?" Adam stepped back from the terrace and looked up at the second floor. A light was on in a room with a small balcony and he wondered if Danielle was in there.

Marcel shrugged, threading his finger through some vines covered with small pink flowers.

"At first it was a land deal that turned sour. Then there was the organic flower farm that I thought would be a nice fit and turned out to be a scam."

Adam didn't comment, figuring the guy must realize how naive he'd been to commit his dollars to projects he hadn't thoroughly researched first. Adam knew a guy back home who had lost the family fortune the same way, investing his money before he'd done his homework. The guy had lost his house, his company, his family. Everything.

"So Les Rêves's assets are…gone?" He couldn't imagine what the news had done to Danielle. Thinking about her sitting alone upstairs grappling with that news made him angry at her brother.

"Not completely. We are financially devastated, perhaps, but not devoid of assets." Marcel released the pink flowers, knocking two to the ground without noticing. "I just wanted to make her aware of the situation before she took on additional commitments for Les Rêves. I thought we'd be able to handle the production for the Dubai retail account if she lands it. God knows we need it. But the more I looked at the books, the more I worried maybe I should tell her first so she might consider an offer to just sell the business outright. I had hoped she would simply take the offer from Panache."

The look of wary hopefulness in the guy's eyes told Adam how far out of touch with reality Marcel remained.

"You've got to be kidding me." Adam yanked on a wrought-iron chair and dropped into it, bowled over by how blind a person could be. "Didn't you hear her a minute ago? She'll never sell the business. She doesn't care about salvaging any money out of this. She cares about saving a company that means the world to her because it represents a passion she shared with her mother."

"So you won't make an offer for the business?"

"No offense, man, but you might want to back out of her business before you make things even worse. She deserves to be able to figure out where to go from here on her own."

Adam shook his head. He half wished he wouldn't win the International Markets account now. Except that Danielle wouldn't appreciate winning a bid he rigged. And he couldn't be the kind of guy that sold out his own family the way Marcel had.

Damn it.

If he bought Les Rêves, Danielle would be as devastated as her finances. But if he won the Dubai account with Ahmed, he'd essentially be running her out of business anyway.

"In that case, maybe it's best I leave." Marcel pulled a set of keys out of his pocket.

"Why? So you can run out on her now, too?" Adam tossed the same accusation in Marcel's face that the guy had launched at him earlier.

"She doesn't want me here." Marcel tossed the keys in the air so they glinted in the porch light.

"I'm sorry to say that's one thing we seem to have in common."

CHAPTER FIFTEEN

ADAM LISTENED TO Marcel's sports car roar away into the night, then slumped down into a wrought-iron chair on the front terrace, not sure where to go next.

He would be on *Alexandra's Dream* tomorrow afternoon for his final meeting with Ahmed. He'd made sure the family's pilot remained on duty nearby to take him to Marseilles, where the ship docked next.

But should he leave now? Danielle obviously didn't want to see him in light of her business problems, but at least he had uncovered the mystery about why she'd stood him up for their date in Ville-franche earlier. She hadn't been jet-setting around the globe for the hell of it. She'd been immersed in damage control.

Which left him…where?

He tipped back in the chair, balancing the wrought-iron seat on two legs while he breathed in the scent of the night. Flowers bloomed in shiny black pots around the front door, making the air fragrant. Thanks to Danielle, he appreciated the scents more than he would have in the past. He'd sent women flowers more times than he could count, never thinking of the smell or stopping to customize the choice for the woman.

Still, he was nowhere near the expert that Danielle was. She would be able to identify every component of that floral blend winding its way around his senses at the moment. She was a connoisseur in her field, a professional with all the credentials he lacked.

Perhaps that's what made her predicament all the more unfair. No matter how much of an expert she was, she possibly wouldn't land the International Markets account because Adam's industry connections and marketing savvy could bring the retailer a fatter bottom line in a shorter amount of time.

That wasn't his ego talking, although he'd certainly let that run free often enough in the past. He simply knew Ahmed couldn't afford to make the more edgy—and risky—decision.

The fact only reinforced Adam's concern that Danielle hadn't faced her last professional hardship this week. On top of her brother's betrayal, she would be dealing with the loss of a potential account. Of course, maybe she'd be relieved since her brother's schemes might have reduced Les Rêves's ability to fulfill the orders a large account would require.

Whatever the outcome, it would be disappointing for her and might mean she wouldn't be returning to the cruise ship. In which case, Adam figured he'd better make an effort to say goodbye to her tonight.

He felt weight on his chest at the idea, but he wouldn't leave without trying to thank her. Danielle Chevalier had done more than teach him about scents and the perfume business this week. After twenty years of keeping a frenetic pace in the workplace, Adam had learned the benefits of taking a little down time. Danielle had helped him see that pleasure wasn't something frivolous.

It was a vital way to recharge himself, and he refused to miss out any more.

FROM THE GARDEN in the backyard, Danielle could hear someone walking through the house.

Marcel? Or could it be Adam?

She'd heard a car speed away half an hour ago, but she wasn't certain if it was Marcel or Adam. Pausing between two pillars covered in bougainvillea, she sipped a cup of hot tea and listened as she wrapped her arm around herself in her silk pajamas and long robe that were her nod to comfort clothes. She told herself she didn't care who it was walking this way because she didn't particularly want to talk with either of them tonight. Her anger with Marcel wouldn't dissipate for a long time after what he'd done.

And Adam…

She wasn't sure how she felt about his arrival in Paris right in the middle of her professional crisis.

Was he responding to Marcel's call for offers from interested investors? Or had he come for less mercenary reasons?

She didn't know because she hadn't given him a chance to explain himself. But then, her passionate nature had led her astray more than once in the past. She needed to learn to control her emotions better if she was going to pull her company out of this mess.

"Wow."

The masculine voice on the other side of the garden startled her even though she'd known someone was coming, and across the shadowy shapes of overgrown plants and untended fruit trees, Danielle spied Adam's outline in the moonlight.

"You're still here." She walked a path of small mosaic stepping stones she'd made herself as a teenager. The brightly colored rock tiles had been gifts for her mother for birthdays and Christmases for five years, resulting in a path of ten brightly colored stones.

Danielle wished all of life's trails were marked so clearly.

"I'll head out soon." He moved closer, his shadowy outline kick-starting something inside her despite the events of past few hours.

What would it be like to have someone to lean on when life turned rough? That was one experience she'd never had as an adult. The thought made her as uncomfortable as it made her wistful.

"I did not mean to be rude earlier." She ducked

under a low-hanging branch of an orange tree toward the center of the old garden. "I cut you off when you were trying to talk to me and—"

"I don't know all the details, but I gather you've had one hell of a day." The low notes of his voice soothed her.

"My brother seems to have been leading a bit of a double life." She found the fountain at the garden's heart and took a seat on the stone bench across from it, settling her teacup at her feet as she plucked a fragrant wisteria bloom. "I find it frustrating that he could take financial chances with Les Rêves's assets, and yet his Italian sports car is still available for trips around town."

Leaning forward on the bench, she smoothed a hand across the edge of the fountain base, which was shaped like an open shell. A nude Venus reclined in the center, her hair cascading in waves of stone. It was one of her mother's earliest pieces, before she had turned to painting for good. What it lacked in artistic merit, it made up for in emotional appeal and captivated garden visitors.

"What will you do with the company? Did he leave you with enough to continue operations?" Adam joined her on the bench.

The scent of his cologne had faded but she could catch a light hint of hyssop on the night breeze. The warm strength of him beside her bolstered her spirits even though she knew he had come to say goodbye.

So much for having someone to lean on. She

released the silly fantasy as surely as she let a wisteria bloom float away from her grip along the water swirling in the fountain.

"I am unsure until I have an independent analyst come in and make some sense of the books. I will buy out my brother, however. We will never work together again, at least not in a partnership capacity."

Her life would change exponentially from here on. Marcel's betrayal stung bitterly. He had learned about fragrances beside her at their mother's knee. They had shared the same upbringing. The same unconditional love.

"If it's any consolation, I think your brother regrets what he did."

Such thoughts couldn't make their way through the ache of Marcel's betrayed.

"Maybe one day that will comfort me. Today—it does not seem to help."

"I didn't come here tonight because of your brother, by the way." Adam scooped up a jasmine bough that needed trimming. Bending to the branch, he buried his nose among the flowers and breathed deeply.

"You didn't?" She hadn't wanted to believe he'd come all this way to try to buy out her business. And yet, what other reason could there be?

"No. I'd just been talking to Joe before I got your message and he'd been saying—" He released the branch, the jasmine leaves sliding along the ground. "The scent reminds me of you."

The simple compliment soothed her. He might not be here for long, but she couldn't stop herself from soaking up what little time—comfort—she could from him for now.

She broke off a sprig of flowers and tucked it in his jacket like a boutonniere.

"I fell in love with jasmine while I lived in this house. It was my favorite scent until we took the country house and I found a few others that I thought were fair rivals." She backtracked to his earlier remark. "What did your brother have to say when you spoke to him?"

"He'd been reading up on you after our photo appeared in the Italian press."

Things fell into place now, and she wasn't sure she liked this new reason for Adam's appearance any better than the one she'd feared. Her hands fell away from his jacket. Instead of coming to Paris to pick over the remains of Les Rêves, he'd come to test the truth of her party-girl reputation.

"I see. I told you I had a wild side, but you did not believe it until you heard it from your brother. Yet we seem to share the ability to attract gossip. Is it possible you are a man who subscribes to the double standard?"

She rose from the bench, her body tense from deflecting blows all day. She would not have thought that such a small thing as Adam doubting her word would hurt this much. She should be numb by now.

"Absolutely not." His conviction was admirable.

"I told you I don't buy half the crap that appears in papers and I meant it. But I had to wonder why you hadn't really shared your own run-ins with the vultures of the society pages when I told you about mine. You didn't tell me— Hell. You didn't tell me."

Hadn't she? Funny, she remembered things differently.

"I told you I was often misjudged. And I told you I had a wild reputation, but you did not believe me since you saw a more sophisticated woman than your publicity-seeking actress." She shrugged, some of the fire returning to her. She ignored the tiny voice in her head that told her she was using anger to cover a deeper pain. "I cannot help that you did not believe me, and I will not apologize for not trotting out every sordid little tidbit that's printed about me every time I step into the social arena where I conduct most of my business. Now if that's all, I'm going to bed and you can flag down your private pilot and tell him our business here is most definitely finished."

She had a head of steam and was ready to tear through the garden and into the house when his arms snaked around her waist, and preventing her from going anywhere.

"Wait," he said.

"Let go." She spoke through clenched teeth, holding back the anger. And yes, the hurt.

"Listen." His fingers tightened on her waist and she couldn't deny an immediate, physical reaction that was anything but unpleasant.

"Have I not heard quite enough?" She held herself stiff, so many emotions running through her she couldn't tell what she felt anymore.

"No. Because you don't know that I realized I was thinking with my pride instead of my head."

He spun her around to face him, and when she saw the fire in Adam's eyes, some of the stiffness slid from her shoulders.

"Will you come back to the ship after all this?" His grip on her loosened and she realized she didn't want to walk away.

She hadn't given much thought to the cruise, but it would probably be foolish to return to *Alexandra's Dream*. "I've given my final pitch to Ahmed. There is no more I can do but await his decision, which I can do here as easily as there."

"The promise of darts won't lure you back then?" His lopsided smile told her he was teasing and yet—

Did he hope for more between them despite their carefully set ground rules?

"The threat of my business going under is a strong incentive for me to stay. I am not the party girl I am accused of being. I care about Les Rêves."

He absorbed her words slowly, as if he were considering arguing with her. Or, perhaps, trying to change her mind. In the end, however, he simply nodded.

"Then it's a damn good thing I followed you."

"Oui?"

"Yes. Because now at least I'll get to say goodbye."

Her heart constricted at those words, then his lips met hers.

Adam's arms around her blocked out everything but the scents of the blossoms and warm earth. She tilted her head up to receive his kiss, the sweet stroke of his tongue breathing life into her when she felt so defeated. He stirred her as no other man ever had, and with only a kiss. She lost herself in that sensation, allowing the moment to spin out until they were both breathing hard.

"Maybe I should come back to the ship just to gather my things," she heard herself saying, drunk on kisses and the thought of the days she'd miss being with Adam. The nights.

He cradled her face in his hands.

"Then I won't say goodbye yet." His thumb caressed her cheek. "Good night, Danielle. And don't worry about the business. You're too talented to let Marcel's mistakes pull you under."

She wanted to ask him more about that. She could have used a few encouraging words on a day that had all but sucked the life out of her. But when she pried open her eyes in the wake of that mind-drugging kiss, Adam had gone.

AS A LIFELONG COMPETITOR in every area of his life, Adam understood that not every triumph tasted sweet. Some were tainted by coming too easily, and others—like this one—were disappointing because you knew you shouldn't have won in the first place.

Adam had received the call from Ahmed the day after he'd pitched his concept to the retailer. Ahmed had offered Adam the lead contract—a tidy sum that had Joe turning cartwheels. Adam's supporters back in New York raked in a hefty sum from the naysayers who didn't think he could close a perfume deal. Ahmed had told Adam he was awarding a secondary contract to Danielle for a lesser amount of money to distribute the Les Rêves brand in select high-end markets. Ahmed planned to call Danielle at her shop in Nice to seal the deal and fax over the contract.

That was the last Adam had heard about her, since she hadn't put in an appearance on the ship again. Adam hadn't bothered attending the final conference banquet or the industry awards the last night of the cruise. His heart was no longer in the job.

Now, as he sat in his office in New York a week later, he couldn't stop thinking about her. Nor could he get rid of the bitter taste in his mouth left by his business victory.

Sure he'd won the contract. Burns Inc. would be better able to handle his father's retirement with a solid profit-generating account in place for their largest company. The Burns Foundation would profit, too, and had already received a check based on the retainer Adam had received to begin work. Two of the foundation's recipients had called to thank him and their appreciation over the donation had been the highlight of winning the contract.

But thinking about Danielle, and how the loss of

the lead spot with International Markets had to have hurt her business even further, Adam couldn't take much joy in his win. He couldn't have pulled it off without her. She could have let him hang himself with Ahmed the first time they'd met in the wine bar when Adam hadn't immediately realized who the guy was. Plus, Adam had gone on to do one of his most enthusiastic presentations based on the knowledge of perfume Danielle had given him. He hadn't stolen a single idea, of course. But he'd absorbed some of her passion for the product thanks to her ability to describe the compelling aspects of scent so well to a guy who'd spent more time smelling sweat than fragrance.

A banging on his office window hauled him out of his thoughts. Joe stood on the other side of the glass, his suit so damn crisp he looked like he'd just walked out of the tailor's.

At Adam's nod, Joe let himself in the office and automatically turned down the overhead television in one corner that Adam kept permanently on ESPN.

"What gives, bro? Every time I go by your office lately you're out to lunch."

"Funny you should say that because I've ordered in every day for the last week just so I can catch up with the work no one helped out with while I was away." Adam had slept in the office the first two nights, in fact. Life in the penthouse hotel suite was starting to wear on him.

"You know what I mean." Joe dropped into the

wingback across from Adam's desk and picked a pencil out of a cup decorated with tin foil given to Adam as a thank-you gift from a sick little girl he'd visited through the Burns Foundation a few months back. There was a picture of Adam and the girl in a cut-out heart with a lace doily around it. His walls were covered with photographs, handprints and paper chains he'd scored from visits to hospitals and orphanages over the years.

"Hey, at least I'm doing some thinking, which is more than I can say for the man who bet against a sure thing." He turned the conversation around, not ready to answer questions about what happened with him and Danielle. Questions he'd sensed on the tip of his brother's tongue for days.

"You think you can distract me from my purpose that easily?" Joe straightened his tie even though he'd sprawled himself sideways in the chair by now.

Adam willed his phone to ring, but his office remained silent.

"Come on. Spill." Joe drummed his pencil on his knee. "What happened with the *mademoiselle?*"

Joe did a pretty accurate French accent, but it lacked the appeal of Danielle's.

"She went back to work, same as me." He shrugged even though it ticked him off not to have heard from her by now. Didn't she know he wanted to find out how things were going with the business? He'd picked up the phone a dozen times in the past week, but never placed the call simply because they'd had a deal for good reasons. They lived on opposite sides of the Atlantic, and they were both committed to their careers.

Except they'd made plenty of time for each other last week. Danielle seemed skilled at finding ways to relax and have fun no matter how much she loved her work.

"Are you going to see her again?"

"Since when do you interrogate me about women I date?"

"Since you seem to do such a piss-poor job of dating in general when left to your own devices." Joe grinned, picking up the tempo of his impromptu drum solo now that he'd a second pencil involved.

"I don't know if I'll see her again. She's busy pulling her company out of a crisis since her business partner—her brother, by the way—screwed her out of a big chunk of company assets."

Joe straightened.

"Sounds serious."

"Makes you appreciate how fortunate you are to have me, doesn't it?" He thumbed the remote on his corner television to raise the volume, a not-so-subtle signal to his brother their conversation was over.

"You could buy the business, you know." Joe sat up again to reach behind him and tap the off button on the TV. "I checked out the profile on the company a couple of years ago and it's got a great niche even if it's struggling. We could spiff it up, make it rock-solid."

"And milk the charm out of it in the process?" Adam had seen more than enough buy-outs, mergers and liquidations of smaller firms to last him a lifetime.

"Is that what you think we do?" Joe's forehead furrowed.

Adam shrugged. "Don't you?"

"Hell, no. I think we bring a unique perspective to every business we touch. I've been meaning to talk to you about the future, bro, because I'd like to change our focus."

"You want to take Dad's spot, don't you?"

It was the first time he could remember seeing his brother struggle for words. Adam would be lying if he said he didn't enjoy watching the smooth-talker get tongue-tied.

"It's cool," Adam reassured him, realizing how very okay he was with that. It could be his ticket to try some other things. Travel. Work on a few of his own business opportunities after busting his butt for so many years on his father's workload. There had been a handful of businesses that Burns managed that held personal appeal for Adam, including a winery, a small market football team and now, amazingly, the perfume business. But he'd never been able to specialize in the areas he enjoyed because of the corporation's vast diversification.

"I'd never want to take it if you—"

"No, I mean it." The rightness of his brother's ambition settled around Adam for the first time and he felt a weight rolling off his shoulders. He could think of other avenues for his life and his own ambitions. A few jasmine-scented possibilities came immediately to mind. "I wouldn't be opposed to making a few changes myself...."

CHAPTER SIXTEEN

DANIELLE'S SHOP WAS a long way from the port in Villefranche, but she knew when the cruise ships had docked based on the traffic along the streets, and today the store was jammed with people.

To an outsider, Les Rêves looked like a successful business. Danielle knew she was hanging on by her manicured fingernails. But she would keep hanging on, damn it. She had sold off a few personal items in the month since she'd found out about Marcel's mistakes—a car she didn't need, a few paintings her mother had bought from friends who had gone on to achieve commercial success. But she hadn't been willing to part with any of her mother's work and she refused to sell the country house that Danielle had made her home since moving to Nice. Of course, she could just barely afford to keep all sixty-five employees on the payroll. If it came down to the house or the employees, Danielle would find an apartment to rent.

She hadn't even had the heart to displace Marcel from the Paris house, although to his credit he had sold his Ferrari to return a small percentage of the money he'd lost through his bad investments. Danielle was in the process of buying him out and his name had been removed from the list of authorized parties with access to the company's accounts. He would not be able to repeat his mistakes.

For now, contrite, he was manning the front counter along with his teenage daughter from his first marriage—a beautiful girl whose mother had been smart enough to uproot her daughter from Paris and relocate to Marseilles ten years ago. Danielle was touched that Marcel had offered to pay his daughter good wages from his own pocket to help keep Les Rêves in business while Danielle scrambled to stay afloat.

The Paris production operation was now being supervised by Marcel's former assistant, a capable colleague who seemed to be invigorating the whole process. He'd proposed giving tours of the perfume factory, where many of the steps were still done by hand, so that Les Reeves could benefit from Paris tourism. Tours would require little financial commitment from the company and might result in substantial sales in an attached shop. Danielle was thrilled to back the new idea and to see enthusiasm from the employees despite the financial tightening.

Finishing up some paperwork, she was about to help out on the sales floor when a tentative tap came on her office door.

She knew that soft knock was not a man's, and

yet she couldn't help the sense of anticipation she felt whenever a door opened or a phone rang. A foolish fancy since the man she hoped to see lived thousands of miles away and had made it a point to say goodbye to her.

"Danielle?"

The feminine voice was a familiar one although she hadn't heard it in weeks.

"Ariana?" Danielle opened the door with a flourish and embraced the ship's librarian. The two exchanged a few e-mails in the weeks since Danielle's cruise in regard to a business project. "It is wonderful to see you."

"You, too. I'm glad one of my days off landed on the Villefranche port of call so I could pop in to say hello. Business is good, I think." She looked over her shoulder at the crowded store before Danielle shut the door on the noise out front. The scents of essential oils, body lotions and new all-organic fragrances still wafted around the office.

"Business has really kicked into high gear since I convinced the ship's shopping coordinator to recommend our shop as a destination. I could not have done it without your help in pinpointing the right people to talk to." She rooted around her office shelves for the gift box she'd wrapped as a small thank you.

"It was you who did the hard part." Ariana insisted, waving away Danielle's thanks with her easygoing manner.

"Well I could have never navigated the confusing personnel protocol without your guidance. Between that and your advice about who to talk to to pitch new in-room complimentary soaps for Argosy's ships, I am very grateful." She thrust the pink-and-gold wrapped package at her friend, who slid a small backpack off her shoulders before taking it.

"Thank you." Ariana opened the package—an obscure recording of Wagner's Rienzi opera—and squealed in delight. Danielle had not forgotten Ariana's discussion of opera the night they'd spent researching online for resources to use in the Arabian Nights project.

After a moment Ariana set the package aside. "Danielle, could we talk for a minute more? I know you're busy and I have a few appointments of my own, but I came to the store because I have some news you might need to hear."

Immediately on alert, Danielle nodded, gesturing toward the matching pair of gold-damask club chairs across from her antique cherry desk.

"Of course. Please have a seat." Danielle cleared away the gift wrap from Ariana's present and sat, too. "Can I get you some coffee? Or maybe some sparkling water to combat this heat?"

"I'm fine." Ariana smoothed her gray skirt as she took a seat. "I heard from our hotel manager that your Dubai contact booked another cruise for the spring."

Danielle nodded, unsure why that would be a matter for concern.

"*Alexandra's Dream* must have impressed him."

"There's more to it than that." Ariana shifted uncomfortably. "Apparently he's making some preliminary arrangements to use the cruise to unveil a new line of fragrances."

Her stomach knotted as the news took on greater significance. Of course, it could be that Prestige Scents had decided to unveil a new product line totally independent of any ideas Danielle had brought to the table. Certainly, Ahmed hadn't approached her about the Arabian Nights line. Her contract was for Les Rêves to supply existing scents in the United Arab Emirates marketplace while Adam's company provided the lion's share of perfume options specifically to Dubai customers.

"Did he mention what kind of fragrance line this would be?"

Heaven knew she was interested. Had Adam held back telling her about an idea he'd pitched to Ahmed? While it wouldn't have been a strictly unethical decision, she would be hurt to think he'd seen what she was pitching and hadn't fully explained his own original concept.

"Actually, he did. The hotel manager told me the company wants to unveil an Arabian-themed line and specifically asked if our chefs could create banquet food in keeping with the theme."

Danielle could not come close to thinking of a response. She felt as if the rug had been pulled—no, yanked—out from underneath her.

Ariana leaned forward to cover Danielle's hand with her own.

"I thought I should mention it since I helped you with research for just such a line. And while I'm sure your friend would never engage in that kind of corporate espionage, I did think the coincidence was a bit peculiar."

Danielle's eyes burned. This didn't sound like the Adam she knew, and yet—*mon Dieu*. It would not be the first time she had been duped in just such a way.

"Thank you." Those were the only words she could come up with while her heart slowly fell apart. "Thank you for telling me, Ariana. I owe you so much that I can never repay."

"No." Ariana squeezed her hand. "I'm grateful for your friendship."

Danielle returned the squeeze, but her mind was racing. She had no choice but to contact Adam now to discuss the origins of this new line of fragrances.

Before seeing Ariana out, Danielle made plans to meet for lunch next month when the ship docked in Villefranche again.

Marcel hurried into the office uninvited. Their relationship had been patched carefully together only because her brother had extended numerous olive branches to her in the last few weeks. He carried a stack of papers, relegated to being Les Rêves's gopher for as long as he wanted to work in the shop. He did regret his actions, and he'd joined a therapy group.

"Danielle, you need to go over these as soon as

possible." He thrust a stack of papers in her hand. "They're applications for an operations manager to oversee the stores and the company's day-to-day business. If we're going to increase our sales volume, you can't wait to get more help."

She nodded absently, her mind not on work when her heart ached so deeply. How could she have been so wrong about Adam?

"I know." She'd discussed the idea of the operations manager with Marcel strictly as her brother and not as her partner. She suspected he would always want to play some role in the company whether he owned shares or not, and as long as she watched over him carefully, that was all right with her. She would forgive him, but she would never trust him the same way again. "I can look them over now."

"I ranked them in order of the candidates I thought were strongest. The guy on top has been hounding me for an appointment with you if you have time today."

Danielle forced thoughts of Adam and the Arabian Nights line from her mind.

"Is that so?" She spun the paperwork around to read the qualifications of the first applicant. "I have time today, and now that the bank has processed the deposit from last week's sales, I could probably afford to take on a salary for someone who will work hard to generate new—"

She stopped cold as she read the name typed neatly on the first line of the standard application form.

Adam Burns.

"What kind of joke is this?" How could Marcel skewer her heart with childish pranks after all the grief he'd caused over the last few weeks? Had she been wrong to accept his overtures of peace between them?

But Marcel wasn't looking at her. He stood half in her office and half on the sales floor, his attention fixed on the shop door. He waved to someone she could not see.

A touch of panic seized her. Surely he could not have been serious about this so-called applicant wishing to have an appointment with her?

"Marcel." Her whispered word contained a warning note.

"Just hear him out, Dani," he whispered back, holding open her office door and ushering in all six-plus feet of the man she wanted to see and didn't want to see. The man who filled her dreams and yet might have sold her ideas right out from under her.

She didn't know what to say.

Adam removed a pair of aviator sunglasses and tucked them in his shirt pocket. He looked like a gorgeous, wealthy American tourist, the tense energy of a New Yorker apparent in his movement even when he was relaxed.

"If you'll excuse me," her brother interrupted. "I need to get back to the storefront."

Danielle didn't say anything as he left, closing the

door behind him to give Adam and her privacy. She had a déjà vu moment back to that first day aboard *Alexandra's Dream* when Jonathan Nordham had left them alone to get to know each other on an open deck overlooking the sea.

She'd been just as bowled over then, damn it. Shouldn't she know better now?

"Hello, Danielle. Nice place you have here." He gave her a crooked grin that spoke directly to her heart before her head could issue a warning.

Stifling the giddy sensation a woman sometimes felt as a result of a rapid pulse, Danielle vowed she would play this as coolly as him. No acting on instinct and definitely no consultation with her wild side where this man was concerned.

"Thank you. Congratulations on the Dubai account." Perhaps that wasn't playing it as cool as she would have liked, but she needed to find out what was happening there.

"To you, too." His eyes roamed lightly over her, not in a sensual manner so much as in a warm, assessing way that reminded her how close they'd been a month ago. "I hear your fragrances are selling well already in the UAE marketplace."

She took a fair amount of pride in that fact, actually. She allowed herself a moment's pleasure in his recognition of that success. Despite Prestige's fat contract, the company had not found the right personality to attach to the fragrance it wished to launch as its lead scent. In the meantime, Les Rêves's primary scent would be arriving in stores through-out the United Arab Emirates this week.

"I have had healthy reorders so I cannot com-plain." She tried to remember a self-improvement class she'd once taken that called for affirming mantras during times of life stress.

She told herself she was calm and collected. That she did not want to tear off this man's clothes or jump into his arms.

And devil take him, why didn't that self-help tech-nique seem to be working?

Instead, she simply stared into his eyes and hoped he would give her some clue what he wanted and why he was here before she forgot all about her mantras and kidnapped him for a few days. Weeks.

Adam locked gazes with Danielle, ready to give anything to know what she was thinking right now. She had a mysterious quality to her elegance and so-phistication, a veneer of togetherness that hadn't even been cracked the night she discovered Marcel had sold her out. She'd simply excused herself from the situation and retreated upstairs.

Now, as she stood in front of him in her feminine pink suit, he wanted to touch her so badly he hurt and he hadn't even come close to telling her all the things he'd come here to say.

"So what did you think of me as an applicant?" He figured he'd get the discussion rolling since she wasn't exactly leaping into his arms to welcome him to her side of the ocean.

Peering around her office, which was both chic and comfortable, he thought about how different it was from the impersonal high-rise he'd left behind. Here, botanical prints in lavish gilt frames of various sizes added color to pale gold walls. On another wall, an antique baker's cart held a collection of perfume bottles.

"You mean this?" She waved the piece of paper he'd given to Marcel in response to the ad he'd seen for a position with Les Rêves. "I think you found a clever way to make an appointment, but perhaps you should tell me what you really want from me, Adam?"

A-*dam*.

God she killed him. He'd been going crazy thinking about her the last few weeks and now that he was here, he could swear there was a wall two feet thick between them.

He debated the wisdom of putting himself on the line with her when she seemed so aloof. Then again, he'd already taken a huge gamble to show up here. He wouldn't dilute that by holding back now.

"Wait." She held up a hand, cutting him off. "I have reached a point in my life where I do not wish to play games. I must ask you a question first."

"Fire away. I'm all about cutting to the chase." He'd done the same with Joe a month ago when he told his brother his new game plan. Sometimes it worked best to get everything out in the open.

Maybe clearing the air would take away this awkward tension between them so he could tell her why he was here. He'd thought about her so much the last few weeks that it was tearing him up not to be able to just hold her. Taste her. Bury his face in her hair, which he knew smelled like jasmine.

She took a deep breath as she met his gaze head-on, her violet eyes serious.

"I found out Ahmed is booking a cruise to launch a new fragrance line next spring."

Ah, hell. He hadn't meant for her to find out this way.

"Are you sure?" He'd wanted to tell her under different circumstances when they weren't looking at one another as rivals.

"I have it from a very reliable source. Furthermore, the new fragrance line is scheduled to be Arabian-themed." He couldn't miss the wary look in her eyes. "You wouldn't happen to know anything about that, would you?"

"I need to come clean about a few things." He'd hoped to tackle this part of the conversation last, but she'd moved it to top priority. "Maybe we should sit down."

He gestured toward the chairs in front of her desk but she shook her head and pointed toward a window seat overlooking the street. Tourists, locals and cruise ship passengers hurried by on their way to cafés and shops during the lunch hour. Silk drapes in a soft shade of pink were tied back with golden rope, giving the whole room a girly appeal that charmed him. He wondered if she would ever be persuaded one day to pull the shade on the window and the silk curtains to indulge in a private moment on those gold tapestry cushions.

Wordlessly, she slipped off her heels and folded her legs under her in the window seat.

"I am ready, Adam. Tell me what has happened."

He took his seat more slowly, wanting to push aside the tempting vision of window seat intimacies to concentrate on what he had to say. He needed to push the odds in his favor and make sure he didn't upset her. It was a foreign sensation, putting someone else's feelings before his own like this, but it seemed right.

"After Ahmed awarded me the contract we both wanted, he approached me about designing a line of perfumes with distinctly local appeal, preferably with a nod toward the Arabic world's colorful history."

Her jaw dropped open.

"That was my reaction exactly," Adam assured her, recalling how pissed off he'd been during that phone call. "I knew he was basically asking me to recreate an idea you'd pitched him because I'd seen your sketches. Can you imagine what unhappiness this would have caused if I had been oblivious to your ideas? I would have just gone ahead and done exactly what the client wanted."

"Which was to steal my ideas." Her voice held a cool note.

"More or less." He watched a couple across the street in a crowded café as they fed each other bites of a croissant and wished he could get back to that kind of easy intimacy with the woman beside him.

"So what did you say?"

He could hear the tension in her voice even if he wasn't looking at Danielle. Sitting this close to her, he needed to maintain enough mental distance to say the right things so he wouldn't push her even further away. He'd give his right arm for some of his brother's smooth-talking prowess today.

"I told him Prestige wasn't the kind of company that co-opted other people's ideas for profit."

She nodded, her silky dark hair brushing the lapel of her pink jacket.

"So Ahmed just found someone else to implement my idea."

"Not exactly." He dredged up his plan and hoped she thought it had as much merit as he did. "I suggested he contact you about working in tandem with Prestige so that he could pull from our global marketing office and your original concepts for this line. The rest of our contracts would remain the same, except you'd receive a larger cut as of the spring and Prestige would scale back their role for the launch."

She arched one eyebrow as a group of older cruise passengers walked past with a woman Danielle recognized as *Alexandra's Dream* "expert shopper."

"You lobbied for a more lucrative contract for Les Rêves?" Her tone conveyed her skepticism and he regretted that she'd seen so many shady business moves that she found this hard to believe.

"He wanted to use your idea anyway." The guy would have felt no compunction about taking all of her carefully researched fragrance names and packaging ideas, not to mention a few of her core scent bases for the line. "I made it clear I wouldn't support that kind of corporate backstabbing and he seemed to understand my position."

She held herself very still for a moment and he could almost hear her searching for a hidden agenda. Finally she acknowledged his efforts with a slight nod.

"That was very—generous of you." She waved out the window at the shopping coordinator. The woman had put Danielle's shop on her list of recommended spots to visit, increasing the traffic in the Nice story to almost double.

"Your ideas deserve to be carried out with you behind them, Danielle." He'd admired her passion for perfume, her dedication to her business, ever since they'd met. "You worked hard for this opportunity."

"But I would not have had it without your help." She didn't seem in a hurry to finish their conversation, even though the store sounded busy. "I know that business deals are not always fair."

"Neither are shipboard flings that are cut short, but what can you do? Life has a way of interfering."

Some of the stiff tension seemed to fall away from her shoulders.

"Did you come all the way to Nice to tell me about Ahmed's desire to expand Les Rêves's role in Dubai?"

For the first time since his arrival, Adam detected a hint of softness in her voice. When did he get to know her so well that he could recognize that kind of shift in her moods? The knowledge surprised him even as he counted himself fortunate to have that kind of edge in today's bargaining.

Closing this deal—getting what he wanted from Danielle—would be tougher than negotiating any business agreement he'd ever been involved in.

"I decided to make a few changes after I got back to New York." To put it mildly. He'd had to scrape his brother off the ceiling a few times while Joe freaked out, accusing Adam of being crazier than their old man. "I think I told you that I never felt any real connection to my work other than the foundation, which means a lot to me."

"I remember." She watched him intently now and he hoped he wouldn't come across as crazy in her eyes, too.

"I handed in my resignation to my brother after working for the company part-time through college for four years and full time for sixteen years after that. I'm done."

"You walked away from the family business?" Her eyes widened and he could tell she hadn't seen that coming.

But then, he'd never been good at sharing what was in his head let alone what was in his heart. He took a lot of pride from accomplishing his work, but he didn't go out of his way to talk about it with other people. Maybe because he never had time. Perhaps that would change once he started working in a field he could really embrace.

"Our family business doesn't exactly have the grass roots appeal of what you've got with Les Rêves. Burns Inc. is a massive conglomerate with companies all around the world and I've worked my butt off to make it a powerful contender in the global marketplace. I'll have dividends coming in the rest of my life and the business will give back to the Burns Foundation whether I'm there or not. So I figured it was time for me to find what things in life I was passionate about."

"And what did you come up with?"

Deep breath. Exhale. Time to take the biggest risk of his trip.

"Well, for starters, there's you."

Danielle blinked through all the other news Adam had surprised her with today to focus on what he just said.

"Pardon?" She wanted to be sure she'd heard this part correctly.

"When I thought about what things I was passionate about in life, I came up with you."

The compliment could only be genuine. He had nothing to gain from idle flattery, and he'd already proven he wasn't a man who operated out of selfish motives, judging by his refusal to steal her idea for the Arabian Nights line. In truth, she should have known that all along. His sense of honor and fair play had been evident in the way he respected her wishes when she'd needed space on the ship. In the way he'd sent off his publicity-seeking starlet when other men might have made the most of both the cameras and a willing woman.

Adam Burns was a man to be trusted.

"I am flattered." More than that, she was teetering on the brink of a vast sea of feelings for him, but she was not ready to admit it quite yet. "But you can hardly make a profession of *me*, Adam."

"No. But I can spend some time with a woman who inspires me while I figure out what else in life does. Life seems more interesting when I'm around you, Danielle. There is a lack of cynicism in how you approach the world and the people around you, and I think if I could convince you to let me stick around for a while, I might see what other professional avenues I'd like to explore."

"You don't think I'm a wild child because I attend parties all over Europe?"

"I think you're a canny businesswoman who knows her target demographics."

"You don't think I'm naive about my company for trusting someone who cheated me?" This fear had bitten her hard in the last month, and as long as she had Adam's ear, she thought she'd see what he had to say.

He seemed to have a knack for cheering her up today.

"I think you're wise to focus your energies on your

strengths and you just need to surround yourself with people who will be as dedicated to their jobs as you are to yours." He reached out to her, and when his hand grazed her shoulder she felt her insides go boneless. "No one would ever fault you for trusting a family member. That's an admirable quality, too, even if sometimes the people we care about let us down."

Her heart felt so full, so rich with feeling for him, she could no longer contain it.

"I wanted to rejoin the cruise," she confessed, regretting sorely that she had not been able to take advantage of their time together. "But after I learned Les Rêves would only receive the smaller contract, there was truly no way. I had my hands so full with refinancing and liquidating assets to save the business that it consumed every second of my time until I realized you were already back in New York and I had missed my chance to be with you. To congratulate you. Because no matter how much I believed in my pitch, I respect that you had the better resources for the Dubai account at that time."

She did not want him to view her as a sore loser. She'd just been so overwhelmed by real world concerns that the cruise had felt like a million lifetimes away.

He threaded his fingers through her hair until he cupped the base of her skull. The warmth of trust, of intimacy, of happiness, filled her.

"We were both dealing with a lot of business

issues." He brushed a kiss along her lips. "I missed you those last few days, but they only helped me realize all the sooner that I needed to spend more time with you if you'll have me."

"Here?" She feared sounding selfish after all the ways he'd compromised already. "In Nice? I only ask because the business still flounders until I can secure a couple of stable quarters for earnings."

"Yes, in Nice." He kissed her again, more deeply this time. "Didn't you get my resumé?"

Her train of thought derailed and she tried to put the pieces together again.

"You gave me a resumé. I do not understand why." She kissed him back, honey flowing sweetly through her veins as she thought about having time to explore this feeling and so many others she harbored for him.

"I can afford to be cheap labor while I oversee Prestige's partnership with Les Rêves on this one project. I can put you in touch with our global office and act as a liaison while you develop the scents. At the same time I can check out life on the other side of the pond."

"Even though you have resigned, you would do this for your company?"

He shrugged.

"My stock options are worth more than my salary, and I figured a good way to discover what I want to do will be by taking on work I know I'll enjoy. So I'll work with you for a few months and practice my golf swing. If you want, I can take on some of the day-to-day responsibilities here until you hire someone else. That would give Les Rêves a financial break and would let me develop some more international connections, because I have a feeling that my future is going to be over here."

Joy exploded inside her like a fireworks display of hearts and scented flowers.

"But you are offering to give up so much for me. I can hardly imagine what to give you in return that would match this beautiful sacrifice you suggest."

"It's actually a little more than a suggestion since it's already done. I took a suite at a hotel a few blocks up from here while I test out life abroad. I plan to do some traveling, but I can make my home base here as well as anywhere." He reached for her, gently edging her whole body closer by another inch or two. "Besides, you already gave me something better than any offer to relocate. You gave me your trust."

Something melted inside her at his perceptive words and a deep feeling of connectedness flowed through her. He understood her and he valued her.

"I would not dream of refusing such a generous offer." She could scarcely believe he'd made it. He could live anywhere in the world and do anything he chose with his wealth and talent. Yet he wanted to be here. With her. "Les Rêves would be honored to have you."

"What about you?" He ducked his head into the

crook of her neck and inhaled. "How do you feel about having me?"

"I would be more than honored. I would actually be really excited. Flattered. Thrilled."

She could envision late nights with him in her home, cooking together as the summer shadows grew long and taking meals out on her patio by candlelight. She would show him her garden, the place where she'd learned to love perfume. And they could go to museums to see the paintings her mother had loved best. They could choose new favorites together.

He was about to kiss her but she halted him, her hands on his shoulders, conscious of a small crowd gathering outside her office window.

"There is so much I want to do with you to celebrate this decision. You will not be sorry, Adam."

"I know I won't be." His voice took on a rough edge and she looked forward to being alone with him and creating new memories to add to the ones that had kept her awake at night this last month.

"You know what we're going to do first?" She walked her fingers down his shoulder to rest on his chest.

"Seal the deal with a kiss?"

She nodded toward the crowd of shoppers and a few crew members from *Alexandra's Dream* who had started frequenting her shop in the last few weeks.

"We have a bit of an audience. How about I take

you to a bar a few streets over that boasts this darts game you like so well and we can kiss behind the American jukebox?"

He threw his head back and laughed, the warm sound wrapping her in the promise of good things to come.

"I would love to play darts with you, but I think these people have gathered around your window because they think the French are dedicated romantics."

"I am a respected businesswoman, not a French schoolgirl with her first boyfriend." Still, she leaned closer, more than willing to be convinced.

"You may be a powerful executive, but you are a wild woman at heart."

"Oui." She smiled, falling into the heat of his eyes. "But only for you."

Their mouths met with all the suppressed longing of a month apart, and Danielle's heart opened wide for this man who had taught her to trust again.

Outside, the throng of cruise ship passengers whistled and applauded, perhaps enjoying the idea of love and romance and happily-ever-afters almost as much as Danielle and Adam.

* * * * *

MEDITERRANEAN NIGHTS

*Join the glamorous world of cruising
with the guests and crew of*
Alexandra's Dream—*the newest luxury ship
to set sail on the romantic Mediterranean.
The voyage continues in August 2007 with*
THE TYCOON'S SON
by Cindy Kirk

While cruising aboard Alexandra's Dream
*Theo Catomeri's estranged
father assigns Trish Melrose the seemingly
impossible task of convincing Theo to resign his
shore excursion company with Liberty Line.
But Trish finds herself increasingly less willing
to push the father's demands and increasingly
more attracted to his stubborn son.*

Here's a preview!

"I CAN'T BELIEVE that the government isn't doing more to protect them." Outrage filled Trish's voice and her hazel eyes flashed.

Theo had to smile at her vehemence. He felt the same way but had learned anger without action accomplished nothing. "I know what you mean. We continue to lobby for a ruling to protect wild horses on public and National Park lands. But we can't wait for that to happen. We need to focus on making changes happen ourselves." He leaned forward and his love for these abandoned creatures welled up and spilled over into his voice. "The wild horses of Mount Ainos have no one else. If my foundation doesn't help them, who will? They are on the verge of extinction."

His grandfather had taken him to Kefalonia for the first time when he'd been but a small boy. They'd hiked the mountain above the village of Arginia, and it was there that Theo had gotten his first glimpse of the ponies.

When his grandfather had told him that no one wanted the proud, spirited animals, Theo had felt an instant affinity. Though he knew his grandparents loved him, sometimes he felt as if no one wanted him, either.

Way back then, when he'd been but a child, he'd vowed to help the horses.

Now his childhood dream had become a reality.

"Where do most of your donations come from?" Trish's voice pulled him back to the present.

"Ironically, from tourists." Theo gave a little laugh. "When we do our tours and they learn of the precarious fate of these beautiful animals, they dig into their wallets."

Trish's finger traced an imaginary figure eight on the table top. "It sounds like fewer tours to Kefalonia could mean less money for your foundation." Trish looked straight at him. "By refusing to contract with Liberty, it would seem that you are also cutting off a large source of potential donors to you foundation."

Theo tightened his grip on the cup. "I'm not contracting with Liberty."

To his amazement, Trish didn't back down. She leaned forward and rested both elbows on the table. "Hear me out," she said, raising a hand when he started to speak. "I really want you to sign that contract. It will be good for me, good for you and—"

"I told you—"

"—and good for your foundation," she continued without missing a beat. "As a bonus for signing I will donate the following sum of money to your foundation."

Theo's jaw dropped open at the amount she named. It was at least a year's worth of tourist donations. For a second his mind jumped ahead to what he could do with the money. They could start work on some additional self-filling watering facilities; they could—

"What do you say?" she asked, her eagerness making her words come out fast. "The way I see it, this deal is a win-win for everyone."

She looked so pretty sitting there with the sunlight from the window dancing across her hair and a hopeful gleam in her eyes that Theo was hard-pressed not to give her everything she wanted.

"This money you would donate," Theo said, "where would it come from?"

She paused for half a heartbeat before answering. "From my company."

"Stamos gave you the money, didn't he?" Theo suddenly leaned forward, crowding her, trying not to be distracted by the intoxicatingly sweet scent of her perfume.

She averted her gaze, her hair hiding her eyes from view. "I told you," she said, "I will be the one writing the check."

"The money is coming from him." Equally determined, Theo hammered his point.

"Do you really care who it comes from?" That splash of red was in her cheeks again.

Disappointment coursed through Theo's veins. It was as he'd thought. The redheaded American was in league with the devil. She didn't care about the horses...or him. All she wanted was to get him to bend to his father's will. Theo pushed back his chair. "Our business is concluded." He'd spoken louder than he'd intended.

"I'd sooner strike a deal with Satan himself than enter into an agreement with Elias Stamos," Theo said, keeping his tone low, aware of the curious glances directed their way.

Confusion clouded Trish's gaze. "But why? I'd say in this instance he's being more than fair."

"I don't like being manipulated," Theo said. "And I don't like lies."

Her cheeks reddened as if she'd been slapped. She lifted her chin and her eyes blazed, but when she spoke her words were carefully measured and conciliatory. "I'm sorry you feel that way. That's certainly not the intention of the offer." She rested her forearms on the table. "I want to help you and the wild horses. At least consider the possibility."

Theo could see the desperation in her eyes. She obviously had a lot at stake here. But he couldn't help her, not this time.

His mind had been made up long ago, when he was a little boy. Back then he'd vowed never to have anything to do with the father who hadn't wanted him.

And that was a promise he intended to keep.

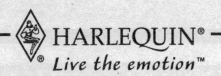

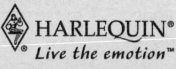

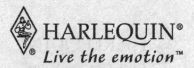

HARLEQUIN®
INTRIGUE®

BREATHTAKING ROMANTIC SUSPENSE

Shared dangers and passions lead to electrifying romance and heart-stopping suspense!

Every month, you'll meet six new heroes who are guaranteed to make your spine tingle and your pulse pound. With them you'll enter into the exciting world of Harlequin Intrigue— where your life is on the line and so is your heart!

THAT'S INTRIGUE— ROMANTIC SUSPENSE AT ITS BEST!

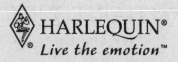

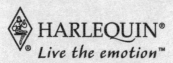

Silhouette

SPECIAL EDITION™

Emotional, compelling stories that capture the intensity of living, loving and creating a family in today's world.

Silhouette

Desire

Modern, passionate reads that are powerful and provocative.

Silhouette

nocturne

Dramatic and sensual tales of paranormal romance.

Silhouette Romantic SUSPENSE

Romances that are sparked by danger and fueled by passion.

SDIR07